My I

Heart
Magazine

Best friends rock!

Cindy Jefferies

USBORNE

For Emma
And for John

First published in 2011 by Usborne Publishing Ltd., Usborne House,
83-85 Saffron Hill, London EC1N 8RT, England.
www.usborne.com

A CIP catalogue record for this book is available from the British Library.

JFMAMJJ SOND/11 02348/1 ISBN 9781409520238
Printed in Reading, Berkshire, UK.

Best friends

Ellie stared at her best friend. "But Hannah! Don't you see? I can't possibly come!"

Hannah folded her arms and tapped her foot impatiently. There was hardly anything that Ellie didn't like about Hannah, but she'd always hated it when she did that.

"I can't believe you don't want to come, Ellie. It's a chance for us both to have a cool holiday *together*! I know it's last minute, but how can you possibly say no? It's *brilliant* that my sister suddenly wants to swan off with her uni friends instead of having a family holiday. We'll have a great time! Besides," Hannah was really piling on the pressure now, "I told Mum you'd *jump* at the chance to come to Spain with us. The room, flight, everything is booked. All we have to do is change the names. If you don't come, Mum will never offer to let me take a friend again."

Hannah's voice was beginning to sound a bit whiny. "Instead of me sharing with my sister we'll be together. It'll be so much fun! You *know* you want to say yes!"

At any other time Ellie would have jumped at the chance. If only she'd known about this much earlier! Yes, it would be wonderful to spend a holiday in the sun with her best friend. She couldn't think of anything better...except... except. Ellie had had her summer all planned out for weeks...no, months before the end of the summer term, and it didn't include a beach holiday with Hannah. It *would* have done, if she'd known in time, but now, it was simply too late. She was working at her fave teen magazine, *Heart*. She'd replied with a thrilled

YES, when she'd had the offer, and she'd already had an amazing time tracking down a reclusive author to interview. Nothing, but *nothing* would make her leave the job early. If she did, it would be very unprofessional. Besides, if she left, she might never be asked back again.

Ellie hated having to choose. Hannah knew how much this work meant to her friend. Ellie wanted to be a journalist more than *anything*, and she couldn't just abandon this amazing job. But Hannah was her best friend, and so Ellie hesitated in spite of herself. Then Hannah tried a different approach. "Come on," she said. "Don't be horrible. Be a proper friend."

Ellie was stung. "Don't say that! Of course I'm a proper friend. But this summer is my chance to make a real impression at *Heart*." She shook the copy she was holding in Hannah's face and Hannah stepped back, pushing it away. "I've already agreed to work all summer," Ellie went on in a rush. "I can't suddenly change my mind now. You know I have a list of celebrities to try and set up interviews with!"

"It's only a couple of weeks out of your precious six," said Hannah in a sulk.

Ellie glared at her. "You're just not listening, are you? Working at *Heart* is really important to me. It could change my whole *life*."

Hannah laughed bitterly. "More important than me? Okay, maybe it's quite glamorous, but it's just a holiday job. They don't even pay you anything. And I thought I was doing you a *favour* by inviting you to Spain. I thought you'd jump at the chance. It's not as if you've had many proper holidays, is it?"

The room suddenly went very quiet. Hannah looked as if she wished she could take the words back, but it was too late for that. Ellie felt ready to explode. Instead, she walked deliberately over to her friend's bedroom door and opened it. Her heart was thumping. She wanted to fling the door wide until it crashed against Hannah's wardrobe. She wanted to sweep all the china ornaments her friend had collected when she was little to the floor, but she didn't. She was so furious she was shaking, but she took a deep breath, and with great difficulty controlled herself.

How *dare* Hannah hint about Ellie's mum's difficulties? Having no dad had certainly made things hard for Georgia, Ellie's mum, but Ellie had almost *never* felt she was missing out. They'd had lots of fun on holidays at home, and it wasn't her mum's fault they couldn't often afford to go abroad.

Ellie turned to look at Hannah, her hand still on the door handle. She wanted to make a clever and wounding parting shot, but she was trembling too much to think of anything to say. She just stared mutely at her best friend for a few seconds, and when she felt angry tears begin to fill her eyes she looked away. Somehow she found her way downstairs and out of the front door, all the time expecting Hannah to run after her, or at least call, but there was silence. They had both gone too far. Their argument was too hurtful to make up easily, and where that left their friendship was anyone's guess.

For the next few days Ellie kept opening her phone to text Hannah, but when it came to it she couldn't do it. She didn't want to be the first to apologize, and there were too many angry words between them for her to simply ignore them and move on. Something had to be said, but what? Maybe Hannah would do the apologizing, and then they could make up, but Ellie's phone stubbornly refused to ring, and no texts arrived.

The more time passed the harder it became. Soon there were only a couple of days to go before Hannah flew out to Spain. Ellie's mum,

Georgia, had noticed that something was wrong, but *she* couldn't put things right.

"Have you and Hannah fallen out?" she asked one evening after work. "She hasn't been round for days."

"She's busy," mumbled Ellie unconvincingly. "Getting ready to go away. And she's annoyed that I can't go with her."

"Well, it is a shame she didn't know her sister was pulling out before you'd accepted the job at *Heart*," said Georgia. "You won't even be able to come with me to drop them off at the airport because you'll be working. But I know how much the job means to you, and I'm sure Hannah will get over it."

It didn't seem very likely, but there wasn't a lot Ellie could do. And she didn't feel like forgiving her friend too quickly for the remarks she'd made about Ellie's lack of foreign holidays. She certainly wasn't about to tell her mum what Hannah had said. Hannah had also implied she was being selfish not to go. Had Ellie been selfish to forego a foreign holiday? A big part of Ellie wished she *could* go. How could denying yourself something be selfish? It was all such a muddle.

It wasn't until the day Hannah was due to go off on holiday that Ellie finally made a move. She still hadn't heard from her friend, but on the bus that morning, on the way to work, Ellie finally sent a text.

Have a great holiday!

She wondered about adding, *See you when you get back*, but what if Hannah didn't want to see her again? Adding that would make Ellie feel too vulnerable, so she didn't. She toyed with the idea of removing the exclamation mark as well. Her finger hovered over the delete button, but in the end she sighed and pressed send instead. For better or worse she'd made the first move. Now it was up to Hannah. The flight wasn't for another couple of hours, so she had plenty of time to pick up the text before she got on the plane and had to turn off her phone.

As the bus chugged along, stopping and starting on the congested road, Ellie thought about Hannah, sitting in the departure lounge with her parents. Hannah's parents were nice. It *would* have been fun to be together, but Ellie still hadn't changed her mind. *Heart* was *the magazine to die for*, and she was committed to working there. If she'd been able to holiday *and* not let *Heart* down...well that would have been perfect! But Ellie was discovering that life was seldom perfect. This was just one of those occasions when you had to make the best of it. Besides, an idea had just popped into her head, and she couldn't wait to test it out on Francesca, the Deputy Editor.

Ellie loved the journey to work. It was exciting catching the buses that took her right into the middle of the city. Once there, she felt she belonged with these sophisticated people, who hurried purposefully into shiny, steel and glass office buildings that rose high into the air on both sides of the streets. In her bag was a pen and her beloved notebook, the one her father had written brief phrases in, shortly before he'd died while on a foreign assignment. That had been before Ellie was born, so she had never met her dad. But having his notebook made her feel close to him, and every day, as she went to work, she thought about the first phrase in the book, *You can do this!* It had become the mantra by which she tried to live her life. It made her feel strong, and capable, and that's what she intended to be.

The bus juddered to a halt at her stop, and Ellie fought her way to the exit. The *Heart* building was only a few metres along the pavement, so she was there within seconds. She paused to gather her thoughts, gazing at the imposing office block with its glass doors.

Then she pushed the enormous stainless steel handle and went in, her heart thumping with excitement. She'd been coming here every weekday since school had broken up, but it was still a huge thrill. *Heart* shared this office building with other magazines owned by the same company, and the spacious lobby was busy with workers making their way to the lifts, the women's high heels tapping noisily on the marble floor.

Ellie hurried to join them. She never knew, from one day to the next, what she might be asked to do, and that all added to the excitement. She really hoped Francesca would love her idea. *Heart* was the coolest magazine *ever*, and the more of an impact she could make, the more Ellie would be right in the middle of it!

She was the same age as most of *Heart*'s readers, and had been a fan for ages. Angel Makepiece, the Editor in Chief hadn't taken long to realize how useful it could be to have

Ellie on board. Not only would they be able to ask her opinion, the readers would love to know that someone their own age was actually on the staff, even though they couldn't pay Ellie until she was older.

Ellie had already interviewed a couple of very famous stars, and had seen her articles in print. The celebrity list that she was working her way through was full of the biggest names in music, fashion and film, but some of them were too busy to be interviewed, which was why Ellie hoped that Francesca would like the idea she'd just come up with. She intended though to wait for the right moment to mention it. Francesca would have to *love* her idea to give Ellie permission to go ahead, and Ellie wanted it to have the best chance of being accepted. So, for now, she hugged it to herself until the perfect opportunity came up.

As she went up in the lift, Ellie checked her phone before she switched it to silent. Angel absolutely hated mobile phones going off, and anyone who forgot to switch to silent was in big trouble.

There was no text from Hannah, but her plane wouldn't have left yet. There was still plenty of time to hear from her, so Ellie refused to feel sad. Instead, she put the phone away in her bag, and smoothed down her skirt and top. Now she was ready for anything!

Questions!
Questions!

Heart's editorial office was on the third floor. Ellie was greeted by a cheerful smile from Debbie Wu, the receptionist, and a scowl from Piano, Angel's PA, who had never tried to pretend that she liked Ellie. That was probably because Ellie's Uncle Patrick had got her the work experience in the first place. Ellie had long ago decided to stop taking any notice of Piano's hang-ups, especially the way she tried to insist that everyone pronounce her name Pea-Are-No. Ellie had discovered that it didn't matter how friendly she was, Piano was never nice back, so there was no point in worrying about it.

Francesca Mosse was much more pleasant than Piano, although she was almost as exacting as Angel. Neither of them would allow anything to weaken *Heart*'s place as *the* top teen magazine, but while Angel seemed to see the worst in everyone, Francesca managed to coax the best out of all the staff by being kind as well as firm. She smiled as Ellie went to her desk and sat down.

"Good morning, Ellie."

"Morning," said Ellie, returning her smile, opening her laptop, and logging on to the system. Now wasn't the right time to mention the idea...maybe later, when Francesca took a coffee break.

"Do you fancy having a go at compiling a quiz for the next issue?" asked the Deputy Editor.

That sounded fun. Ellie smiled eagerly. "Yes please!" Then she paused, and glanced at Piano. "But doesn't Piano usually do them?"

"Yes," said Francesca. "But Piano is quite busy researching an article, so it would really help if you'd be willing to give it a go. I've emailed you the template. You can access all the questions, and pick a selection of those for your quiz."

Ellie was puzzled. "You mean the quiz questions aren't made up especially for each issue?"

Francesca smiled. "Well, the most popular subjects for quizzes are friends, fashion sense and boys. There's a limit to the number of different questions you can sensibly ask about them, so, instead of starting from scratch every time, we work from a pool of standard questions and update them as necessary."

"Oh," said Ellie, not sure how she felt about that.

"If you think about it," said Francesca, seeing Ellie's expression, "the questions *will* probably be brand new for most readers because they'll have been too young to read the magazine the first time the questions came around."

"And they'll most likely have moved on to a magazine designed for adults like *Soul*, our sister magazine, by the time the questions come around again," mused Ellie.

"You've got it," said Francesca. "You'll find you have to update them. That's your main job really, to make them sound fresh. The original questions were compiled under the guidance of a psychologist, and it's important to stick to her template. These quizzes are supposed to be fun, and it's important that we don't upset readers by making them too harsh, or by giving bad advice." She smiled at Ellie. "Don't worry. It sounds more complicated than it is. The psychologist has done all the hard work for you. All you have to do is bring them up to date. They *will* be new by the time you've tinkered with them."

"Okay," said Ellie.

"If you come horribly unstuck I'm sure Piano could find a bit of time to give you a few pointers, but I think you'll find everything you need in the file." Francesca turned back to her screen.

Piano looked at Ellie. It was clear from her expression that she didn't consider Ellie capable of coping unaided with one question, let alone the usual ten they had in their quizzes.

But Ellie had always loved the quizzes in *Heart*. As a reader, before she'd had any hopes of working for the magazine, she and Hannah had totally enjoyed each one, and sometimes they'd even made up their own fun questions for each other. Ellie was determined not to let Francesca down.

Ellie looked at her email inbox and found a new message from Francesca labelled "Quiz". She opened it eagerly. New challenges were great! But when she read the email, Ellie wasn't quite so sure.

What sort of friend are you?

Ellie stared at the question at the top of her screen. Almost any other subject would have been fine, but she wasn't sure she wanted to examine friendship at the moment. It was a bit too close to what she was going through with Hannah. She rummaged in her bag and checked her phone. No messages, and unless the flight had been held up, Hannah would certainly be airborne by now.

She picked up the pencil next to her laptop and sucked the end of it. If the quiz had been about clothes, or make-up, animals, music... anything else would have been fun. But this... still, she couldn't back out now. She put the pencil down again and read what was on her screen.

To follow the *Heart* magazine template she had to choose ten questions. There would be three possible answers to each question, and in the end, the readers should be able to tell if they were:

A. *Real Softies*

B. *Well Balanced*

C. *Tough Cookies*

Could she do this without ending up feeling really down? Of course no one was supposed to take these quizzes too seriously. They were supposed to be fun, to be done over lunch with a gaggle of friends. But her friend wasn't around to giggle with, and Ellie felt sure that compiling this particular quiz was going to make her feel uncomfortable and force her to re-examine her own behaviour. But then she remembered her mantra, and told herself not to be such a wimp. She simply needed to swallow her personal feelings and get on with it!

She took a deep breath, opened the folder of questions and clicked on the "Friends" file.

There were loads of questions and answers, so all she had to do was choose ten, and rephrase them. She picked one and studied it. *You and your best friend have applied for tickets for your fave TV programme. She gets one but you don't. What do you say to her?* That was easy. She freshened it up by making it tickets for a sell-out gig instead. And it was simple to fiddle with the answers to make them work. It was going to be okay.

"Don't make a mess of updating. It would be just like you," said Piano.

Ellie looked towards her crossly. "I won't!"

Piano didn't sound convinced. "Only, loads of our readers turn to the quiz page first. I don't want you ruining the magazine for them by making it too childish."

Francesca didn't look up from her desk, but she must have been listening. "Give Ellie a break, Piano," she said mildly.

Piano scowled, but said no more. Ellie sorted

out a couple more questions and felt pretty pleased with herself. It was going well. Then she came across one that didn't need much updating. *Your best friend asks you to go on holiday with her, but you've already said you'll do something else.*

She stared at the words in front of her and gave a huge sigh. Oh dear. What should she have said?

Do you:

A. Agree straight away and cancel your other plans.

B. Tell her that you'd love to another time.

C. Say you have more important things to do.

She was very afraid that the answer she'd given to Hannah fell under the category of "C".

Ellie stifled a groan. She risked a glance in Piano's direction, but Piano was hard at work on her article and hadn't noticed Ellie's distress. Well, thank goodness for that! Ellie reached into her bag and brought out her phone. There was still no text. By now, surely, Hannah's plane would be far away. Ellie looked out of the window. As she gazed at the sun shining on buildings she saw a plane in the distance. It must have just taken off from the airport, because it was climbing steeply up into the sky. She could have been doing that, instead of sitting here.

Piano's voice jerked her out of her reverie. "I suppose you've forgotten the coffee run, as usual."

Ellie summoned up as much dignity as she could, turned away from the window and stared at Piano. "Of course I haven't." She wasn't being strictly truthful. She didn't *usually* forget. Piano's remark was just Piano being typically sniping, but on this occasion the coffee run *had* almost slipped Ellie's mind. It was only when checking her phone just now that she'd realized how late it was. She'd spent longer than she'd thought working on the quiz. Still, she was in plenty of time to fetch the mid-morning coffee order, and there was no need to rush. That would only make Piano crow. Ellie ostentatiously typed *Q.5.* on her laptop before saving the file and closing the lid. She took her bag and left the office.

Fetching the coffee was the job of the lowliest member of staff, but Ellie didn't usually mind. If she was in the middle of writing an article it could be annoying, but today she was only too pleased. Coffee time meant an opportunity to mention her idea to Francesca, preferably when Piano was out of earshot so she couldn't rubbish it.

Going out into the busy street, she turned right, towards Coffee! Coffee! Invariably, when she was on this errand she felt a delicious sense that while *she* knew that she was working for one of the most popular teen magazines in the country, and had met and interviewed some very famous people, none of the passers-by had a clue who she was, or what she did. It made her feel secretly special, and she wanted to giggle.

While in the queue at the coffee shop, Ellie gave her new idea some serious thought, so she'd be ready to explain it to Francesca. She'd been trawling through some celebrity websites recently, looking for inspiration, when she couldn't help noticing how some people of about her age were included in quite a few of the shots. They were the children of major film stars, or musicians who were big in her mum's day, and were still touring. Some of these teenagers were already stars in their own right, but others seemed to slink along behind their parents, looking grumpy, embarrassed or just plain fed up. Ellie wondered what it would be like having such famous parents. Was it cool being part of the media frenzy, or did they wish it would all just go away? If they wanted to follow their parents into stardom was it made easier for them, or harder?

Ellie had come across a picture of the movie star Elizabeth Broadstairs. The caption said she was arriving in New York with her daughter. For a second Ellie hadn't even *noticed* the daughter, Albion. While Elizabeth seemed to revel in the limelight, striding through the airport, accompanied by huge amounts of luggage, her daughter Albion was dragging along in the background, hiding behind an enormous pair of sunglasses and a floppy hat. While she'd been thinking of Hannah and *her* parents waiting for *their* plane, something had clicked. Why not interview the daughter? If she could persuade Albion to talk she might have a really interesting piece. She could see it now. *My Life with my Famous Mum*. If Ellie presented the idea well, Francesca, and hopefully Angel, would see that it was a perfect interview for Ellie to do!

She hurried back along the street with the coffee order as quickly as she could. In the office she put the tray down on her desk and took Angel's through to where she was busy working in her own, opulent office. Ferdinand, Angel's little dog, was curled up in his basket by the side of her desk. Later on it would be Ellie's job to take him out for his walk, but for the moment he seemed happy. He wagged his tail at her a couple of times and sighed noisily before closing his eyes and covering his nose with his paw.

Angel barely acknowledged Ellie or the coffee, and Ellie didn't hang around. She didn't want to risk pitching the idea to Angel without running it past Francesca first.

Back at her desk, Piano and Francesca had already helped themselves to their drinks. Debbie preferred to make her own tea in the office, and so that left one paper cup on her desk – a latte, which was Ellie's.

As soon as Piano went back to her desk and started to work, Ellie seized her chance. Making sure her back was to Piano, so that hopefully she wouldn't be able to overhear, Ellie went to Francesca, who was taking a few seconds to enjoy her drink.

Quickly, Ellie outlined her idea to the Deputy Editor. "So, you see it would be perfect!" she said, letting her enthusiasm show. "There may well be all sorts of inside stuff that our readers would *love* to know!"

Francesca sipped her coffee and then set the paper cup down. "I agree that it would be a great story," she said. "But I think the chances of it working are very slim. Most celebrities are zealous about keeping their children's lives private. You probably won't get past the agent, because they'll have instructions to refuse any approach to children."

"But this girl isn't a young *child*," said Ellie. "She's practically grown up...like me."

Francesca smiled. "So she is, but all the same, she's still going to be under eighteen, so the chances are it'll be a blind alley for you." She looked at Ellie's crestfallen expression. "How are you doing with the quiz?"

"Um…I'm pretty well halfway through."

"Okay, well that must be finished first, but afterwards, if you like, see how far you can get with setting up an interview with this girl. If the answer is yes I'll certainly clear it with Angel, but I'm not going to trouble her with the idea unless it looks as if it's going to come off. Is that fair?"

Ellie's eyes lit up. "That's great, Francesca. Thanks!"

"Right then. Finish that quiz by lunchtime, and you can use the afternoon to make contact with Elizabeth Broadstairs's daughter, whatever her name is."

"It's Albion," said Ellie, quick to demonstrate that she already knew about her subject.

Francesca shook her head. "Albion Broadstairs? Poor kid," she muttered to herself before dismissing Ellie with a wave of her hand and getting back to work.

Ellie was thrilled. True, Francesca had thrown up a possible problem that Ellie in her haste hadn't thought of, but she'd been given the go-ahead to try, that was the important thing. She did have to finish the quiz first though. She took a gulp of coffee and raised the lid of her laptop. *Question Five*, she thought to herself breezily, *here I come!*

Your best friend has bought a dress that looks awful on her. Do you:

A. Tell her it looks lovely.

B. Tell her it's not the best she's ever bought and if she decides to return it, you'll happily go with her.

C. Tell her it looks dreadful.

That was good, but she could change dress to tunic and leggings, or maybe shorts and leggings. In Ellie's opinion, they definitely didn't suit some people! Ellie and Hannah had always been good at helping each other with clothes, and Ellie knew that if they had been doing this quiz together they would both have answered honestly and helpfully. There was no point in saying something looked cool, if it didn't. As the clothes looked totally awful, the right answer had to be B. A true friend would never be untruthful about that sort of thing. It would be far better to get her money back and spend it on something that did suit her. And it usually helped to have a friend to give an opinion when buying clothes.

Ellie took another gulp of coffee. Honestly was important as well as loyalty. Hannah *had* to understand how much this job meant to her. Surely she would, given time? Meanwhile, Ellie was determined to crack on and get a scoop for the magazine once she'd finished the quiz. And when the summer was over, she'd make it up to Hannah. She didn't know how, but she'd find a way, somehow. For now though, she had a job to do!

3
Ellie's big idea

Ellie didn't manage to finish the quiz before lunch. She had to take Ferdinand for his walk, and Angel told her to collect some dry cleaning while she was out. Ellie wouldn't have minded, but the dry cleaner's was in the opposite direction to the park where she walked Ferdinand. It wasn't far, but it ate into her time, and she couldn't help feeling just a *little* resentful.

"Honestly," she grumbled to herself, putting Ferdinand's lead on after his run. "It's not as if I'm not doing something *useful* in the office. Why does it always have to be *me* doing all these jobs?" Ferdi wagged his tail in response, and Ellie sighed. She knew the reason really. As the most junior member of staff of course she was expected to run errands.

And Ellie was too excited about trying to get an interview with Albion Broadstairs to stay miffed for long. Even so, there was such a lot of dry cleaning to carry back she almost had to make two trips. "Angel's cleaning bill must be enormous," she said to Ferdinand as they struggled into the lift.

When she got back to her desk, Ellie soldiered on with the quiz. By lunchtime there wasn't too much to do, and so, by eating lunch at her desk, and working steadily she soon got it finished. She emailed it to both Francesca and Piano, feeling very pleased with herself. There was still time to find out who Elizabeth Broadstairs's agent was and give them a ring before the end of the day. Ellie googled the actress's name and trawled through the long list of websites. It was easy to get distracted by all the pictures, fan sites and news items, but it was all valuable research. She stopped at a picture of Elizabeth snapped outside her daughter's school. For once she wasn't smiling, and Albion had her head ducked down, looking away from the camera. It must be lovely, thought Ellie, to be the centre of attention when you wanted it, but horrible if you didn't. She was sure she could conduct a brilliant, in-depth interview with Albion. It would give the girl a chance to say how she felt about having a famous mother. All the highs and lows of her life would be described at last. If Ellie was Albion, she was sure she'd jump at the chance to have her say!

Totally fired up now, Ellie added "agent" to the search box and the computer obligingly came up with the agency's website. It was a large company, with lots of big-name clients, so it took a few minutes to match one of the many agents with Elizabeth Broadstairs. As soon as she found the name she dialled the agency's number. Her heart started thumping. All she had to do was convince the agent, Grant Thomas, that it was a good idea to interview Elizabeth's daughter, and she'd be away!

Ellie refused to be put off by the switchboard, and insisted on speaking to Grant. She tried to sound so confident that the person on the other end would assume that she'd spoken to him before. Eventually she was told that she was being put through to his office. Her heart started thumping, and she took a deep breath. But the telephone wasn't picked up by a man. It was a woman on the other end of the phone.

"Grant Thomas's office."

Ellie swallowed nervously. This must be his receptionist, or his PA. She wasn't home and dry just yet.

"Could I speak to Mr. Thomas, please?" said Ellie.

"In connection with...?"

"In connection with Albion Broadstairs."

"I'm sorry, we don't have anyone of that name on our books."

"But…" Ellie struggled to think of what to say. "But you represent her mother…don't you?"

"Yes. We do."

"Well…" she spoke in a rush. "Could I speak to him about her then?"

"Mr. Thomas is very busy."

"I think he'll want to know about this," said Ellie. "I'm calling from *Heart* magazine."

She heard what might have been a sigh from the other end of the line, and then the PA spoke again. "One moment, please."

"Who am I speaking to?"

It was a man's voice. Grant Thomas at last! Ellie rushed to speak. Everything depended on how she presented herself. She must get it right. "My name is Ellie Ixos," she said. "I'm from *Heart* magazine and I would like the opportunity to speak to Albion Broadstairs because—"

"Ms. Broadstairs's daughter doesn't give interviews…"

"But, if I were her, I mean—"

"And if you read our website properly you'd know that." He paused. "Are you still at school?"

"Yes…which is why I thought it would be a good idea…"

Ellie crossed her fingers, bit her lip and closed her eyes. If only he would say yes. She was sure he was wavering.

"I'm sorry. Ms. Broadstairs's instructions are quite clear. No interviews." His voice softened. "Nice try, my dear, but you'll find that lots of the stars feel the same way about their children's privacy."

"That was why—"

But it was no good. He'd hung up. She was speaking to herself.

Slowly, Ellie replaced the phone. It had been a good idea. No, a *great* idea, and in spite of Francesca's doubts she'd been almost sure that she could pull it off. Well, she'd been wrong. All she wanted to do now was to go home, but it wasn't time yet. She couldn't crawl off like a dog with her tail between her legs! She sneaked a glance in the direction of Piano's desk, thinking how fortunate it was that Piano didn't know what had happened. Unfortunately, Piano looked up at the same moment and caught Ellie's eye.

"Ellie. Over here a moment." Ellie's heart sank. What could she want? Surely she hadn't overheard any of that phone call? She got up and went reluctantly over to Piano's desk, dreading being teased.

"Now you've sent me the quiz questions you must have time to take on another job."

It was just as well Ellie didn't ever expect praise from Piano, because she didn't get it.

"So they're all right?"

Piano frowned. "They'll have to do, I suppose. I'm too busy to make them better." She paused. "Anyway, the Fashion Department is doing a piece on plaited hair, and Angel thought it would be fun to have a little item on the way plaits have featured in fashion through the ages." She sighed. "It's all very well Angel throwing out these ideas, but they take time to research. Have a trawl through the internet and see what you can come up with. That should keep you out of trouble for the rest of the day."

"Okay," said Ellie, turning to go. Then Piano caught hold of her sleeve.

"You weren't making a personal call, were you?"

"Of course not!" said Ellie angrily.

"Well who were you calling then?" said Piano. "It seemed a very intense conversation. You weren't speaking to a boyfriend, were you?

You know personal calls aren't allowed."

Ellie was furious. How dare Piano spy on her? She had been going to shelve her interview idea, but Piano's prying made her feel obstinate, as well as furious. Why not try some other celebrities who had daughters of the right age? Of course! She didn't need to give up yet. She could make some more "intense" phone calls. That would infuriate Piano. If Piano was going to be so nosy she deserved to be teased. Except it wasn't *really* teasing, not at all. Ellie would be totally within her rights to keep ringing people until she made her idea work. It was Piano's problem, if not knowing who Ellie was calling infuriated her. She glared icily at Piano. "It was a call Francesca knew I was going to make," she said coldly, before stalking back to her desk. She plonked herself down in her seat and fumed silently. She'd show Piano that she could do more than refresh quiz questions, fetch coffee and research plaits. She also had brilliant ideas, and could carry them through… she hoped so anyway. She'd find a way. All she needed was a lucky break.

Meanwhile, she had work to do, and if she didn't want more remarks from Piano she'd better get on with it.

4
Plaits and personalities

That evening after work, Ellie spent some time at home on the internet, researching famous people's children, and looking for likely candidates for her proposed interview. It wasn't easy. She wanted to interview a girl, because it would be fun to talk about clothes and make-up, as well as privacy, and being the daughter of a famous star. But she needed a teenager, available in London, and not already famous in her own right. It was a behind-the-scenes interview Ellie wanted. Added to that, they had to have parents who didn't mind them being interviewed. It wasn't easy at all.

"It's so annoying," she muttered to herself. "Albion would have been perfect."

By the time she was ready for bed, Ellie had a shortlist of four possible candidates. She jotted the names down in her notebook and thrust it into her bag, ready for the morning. Before she turned out her light she checked her phone one last time. Hannah would be in Spain now, and if she'd forgiven Ellie for not going with her she would surely have texted to tell her what it was like. There was no text. And maybe the hotel didn't have much of an internet connection, because Hannah hadn't been on Facebook, either. Ellie sighed, and put her phone by her bed.

She switched out her light and lay down. She wished she *was* in Spain with Hannah. Today hadn't exactly been one of the best days ever. Working at *Heart* was usually so exciting, but somehow today it had lost some of its gloss. It was probably just because she missed Hannah, and because her big idea had so far come to nothing, but she couldn't help the way she was feeling. For the first time, she found she wasn't particularly looking forward to going to work in the morning. Finding information about plaits was tedious. She even wondered if Piano had made up the project just to keep her away from more interesting work. She was also worried that she'd draw a blank with the four names she'd found as possible interviewees. And instead of worrying about this she could have been on holiday! What was she trying to prove, pretending to be a journalist? Maybe she just wasn't cut out for it. Grant Thomas had called her "my dear" and that had made her feel about six.

Then Ellie told herself not to be so stupid. She couldn't expect everything to go her way all the time. She had to *work* at being a journalist. Her father had worked at it for years. He hadn't suddenly become a renowned war correspondent by giving up at the first hurdle.

She reached out of bed and felt for her bag. She drew out the old, black notebook that had been his and clutched it fiercely. Ellie had never known her dad. He'd been killed on assignment shortly before she was born, and this notebook was all she had of his. She turned over the pages thoughtfully. Here was something she hadn't noticed before. If *you only have one direction, don't make it backwards.*

She read it several times, but it didn't help. She wished she could ask him precisely what he'd meant. After brooding about the phrase for a few more minutes she put the notebook back in her bag and turned out the light. Her dad wasn't there to help. Neither was Hannah. She didn't want to bother her mum, so she was on her own. Why did she suddenly feel that her life was going wrong? She was usually so positive, but somehow that had all gone. *Maybe*, she thought without much hope, *I'll feel better in the morning.*

In the morning Ellie *did* feel better. Suddenly, her dad's words seemed to make perfect sense. He was telling her not to regret the past. She couldn't rewind what had already happened. Life didn't work like that. She had to cope with what she'd got. So, she had to go on, and leave worrying about herself and Hannah until she was in a position to do something about it. Forward was the way to go in life, which in her case at the moment meant going all out to find a good person to interview, and not to allow herself to become defeated. She wanted to be an excellent journalist? Well she'd have to get on with it then!

Giggling at her own pep talk, and relieved that she felt so much better, Ellie ate a good breakfast, chatted happily to her mum, and then strode down the road to the bus stop, feeling strong and determined. Because of an abnormally bad traffic jam she was a few minutes late into work. Piano did her usual long-suffering, eye-rolling act. Ellie had to stifle a laugh. It seemed so silly in her new, bouncy mood that she'd ever allowed Piano to get under her skin.

Almost immediately, even before Ellie had opened the lid of her laptop, Francesca sent her down to the basement with a parcel for Sophie to deal with.

"Can you tell her it's urgent?" said Francesca. "She'll need to get it biked round."

"Okay. I'll tell her." Ellie was pleased to be able to go down to the post room. Sophie had always been a great friend. What's more, she had a gorgeous boyfriend, Flynn, and Ellie always enjoyed hearing the gossip about their life together.

Sophie was busy sorting the mail, but she stopped what she was doing when Ellie arrived, and took the parcel.

"Hi!"

"Hi," said Ellie, and she explained about the parcel.

"Hang on then, while I ring the courier."

As soon as Sophie had arranged for the parcel to be collected, Ellie asked her how life was treating her and Flynn.

Sophie smiled. "Well, I sold another of my pots to a collector the other day. How about that?"

"Well done," said Ellie. When Sophie wasn't being the post girl she made wonderful studio pottery and was just beginning to get known for her work.

"Thanks," said Sophie. "Unfortunately, the day didn't end as well as it began."

"Oh no, what happened?"

"Nothing to do with my pottery, thank

goodness, but honestly… Friends!"

"What?" said Ellie.

"Oh it's just that my two best friends have taken it into their heads that Flynn and I should be thinking of getting married. I mean really!"

Ellie giggled. "Perhaps they want to be bridesmaids."

Sophie stared at her. "Ellie! You are *so* right. We had a girls' night out, and they started counting up how long Flynn and I have been together. Then they started arguing about which of them would get to be chief bridesmaid. I mean…how stupid. We don't even *want* to get married yet…if ever."

"So what happened?" said Ellie.

"Well, I got cross about them discussing me like that and told them that if Flynn and I *did* ever get married we wouldn't be asking them to be bridesmaids."

"Oh dear," said Ellie. "What did they say?"

Sophie propped her chin on her hands and sighed again. "I only meant that I wasn't into having bridesmaids and all that stuff, but they didn't take it like that. It stopped them arguing with each other, but they got into a huff with me instead."

"I expect they'll soon forget about it," said Ellie.

"Probably," said Sophie. "But what a waste of a good night. It seems that sometimes it's so easy to fall out about the smallest things."

"That's true," said Ellie.

"So what about you and Hannah?" said Sophie. "You heard from her yet?"

Sophie was the one person at *Heart* who Ellie could really confide in. Ellie had told her all about her fight with Hannah, and Sophie had been very sympathetic. Ellie shook her head. "Still no text," she said sadly.

Sophie gave her a hug. "Try not to fret about it," she advised. "There's nothing you can do for now. And if she's a really good friend she'll realize that you couldn't do both things. You had to choose what was right for you. I'm sure that time will heal. In fact, I bet you as soon as Hannah arrives home she'll be on the phone, wanting to tell you all about her holiday."

"I hope so," said Ellie.

Sophie gave her a sympathetic smile. "Don't worry about things you can't change," she said. "Time enough to think about it when Hannah comes home."

"You're totally right," said Ellie. "In fact I told myself the very same thing this morning." She took a deep breath. "Give me some more gossip to stop me brooding."

"All right." Sophie bit her lip, thinking hard. Then she grinned. "I'll tell you the latest that my friend Claire told me. You know she works in that big hotel?"

"Yes?" Ellie leaned against the wall and prepared to be entertained. Sophie had shared a couple of Claire's stories with her in the past, and they'd always been amusing.

"Well the lead singer from Steel Vortex is staying there at the moment. Have you heard of Steel Vortex?"

Ellie indulged in her own version of Piano's eye rolling, but she was only teasing. "Duh! Of course I have. You mean the heavy-metal band."

Sophie nudged Ellie in protest. "Well I'm not much of a metal fan so *I* didn't realize who they were. I suppose you know the lead singer's name is Rocky Steel then? What sort of a name is that? Surely it must be made up?"

Ellie giggled. "I think it's like a stage name, Sophie – you are so out of touch!"

"Okay. It's a stage name," said Sophie. "But Claire says he's as crazy as his name. When he got to the hotel he wanted to check in his pet pythons. Imagine! Apparently they're huge, and need heat lamps and all sorts of stuff.

He appeared at the front desk with one around his *neck!*"

"It could have eaten someone's dog!" said Ellie.

"And Claire has a terrible fear of snakes," said Sophie. "She had a total panic attack. The duty manager had to get her to breathe into a paper bag to calm down while he sorted it out."

Ellie giggled.

"But how about this?" went on Sophie. "Rocky has his fifteen-year-old son staying with him as well as the snake. His name is Joe Steel."

"I like that name better," said Ellie.

"Apparently he's really cute too. Polite, good-looking, nothing like his dad, who looks as if he's been sleeping under a hedge for years." Sophie grinned at Ellie. "You see, there's always someone worse off than you. What are a few problems between friends compared to being lumbered with a father called Rocky Steel?"

"You're right," said Ellie. She gave Sophie a grateful smile. "Thanks for giving me a boost. I must get back upstairs now or I'll have to do the morning coffee run before I've even opened my laptop!"

"Piano will be rolling her eyes again," said Sophie, who had experienced the treatment first hand in the past.

"Oh no!" said Ellie, in mock horror.

"Join me for lunch if you like," said Sophie, picking up a bundle of post to deliver.

"Okay," said Ellie. "See you later."

Back in the editorial office, Ellie logged on and reluctantly got back to researching plaits for Piano. She couldn't *really* believe that Piano had made the job up, but Ellie would much rather have been doing her own work.

Readers aren't going to be interested in the history of plaits, she thought. *They're just going to want to see some different styles, and instructions on how to do them.*

But, in spite of her opinion, Ellie did get quite interested as she carried on with the research. Soon she had a picture of a Chinese girl, a group of ballet dancers, an English teenager and a Native American woman, all sporting different styles of plait. She couldn't find much about the history of the hairstyle, but she did come across a picture of a beautiful French plait and added that to the file, thinking that the Fashion Department might like it and come up with some tips on how to achieve the look. Then she emailed the lot to Piano, hoping that Angel would be satisfied.

By then, it was time to fetch the coffee, and after that she had to take Ferdinand out. But once he'd been exercised, she'd have an opportunity to try the possible interviewees she'd chosen last night. She couldn't spend too much time on them. She still had the long list of celebrities that Francesca wanted her to approach over the summer, and so far she had only done one interview on that list, with a highly successful but reclusive author. That had proved to be a huge scoop for the magazine, as the author had turned out to be not one person, but two – a mother and son writing team. Francesca and Angel had been very pleased, and so had Ellie, but that great success had rather set the standard. Ellie knew that Francesca wasn't expecting the same high standard every time, but she also knew that Piano was hoping she would fall flat on her face very soon. Ellie simply had to make the next interview a great one. If only she could find the right person – one who was prepared to talk.

In spite of her determination, by lunchtime Ellie had drawn a complete blank. One agent had been very tempted by the idea of her interviewing the daughter of a TV soap star, but had admitted that no way would his client allow it.

"You're a couple of years too soon," he told her. "Come back when she's eighteen. Then the mother won't be able to stop her daughter from giving as many interviews as she wants. And believe me, she wants to!"

Ellie wondered if she ought to give in, and approach some over-eighteens, but her idea had been to find out what it was like for girls who were the same age as the readers of *Heart*. Feeling stuck, she went down for lunch with Sophie.

"I really don't want to talk to someone over eighteen, because anyone can do that," she explained to Sophie. "It's only going to be special if they're younger."

"So special you can't make it happen," said Sophie, taking a bite out of her sandwich.

"I could try Joe Steel, I suppose," Ellie said thoughtfully.

"That's a good idea," said Sophie. "I bet his dad wouldn't mind. He seems to do almost anything for publicity."

Ellie shook her head. "You'd probably find he drew the line at putting his son in the limelight. Besides, he's a boy. I really want to interview a girl."

"Oh." There was a pause while they both ate companionably. "Why?"

Ellie looked up. "Why what?"

"Why do you want to interview a girl? Come on, Ellie." Sophie was serious. "Why does it have to be a girl?"

5

Sophie's help

Ellie wiped a few crumbs from her mouth while she thought about what Sophie had said. "It would be fun to talk about fashion as well. Children of celebrities have so much money sloshing around. What do they think about designer clothes? Do they have to wear things that complement their famous parent's image... that sort of thing. But I suppose that could apply as much to a boy as to a girl."

"It could," said Sophie. "And you know that Joe Steel and his famous father are in town... you even know exactly where they're staying!"

Ellie looked at Sophie. "And *Heart* readers do love reading about good-looking boys. *Is* he really that good looking, Sophie?"

Sophie smiled. "Well, Claire thinks so, and I reckon she's quite a good judge. Her boyfriend is *gorgeous*! And of course she's on good terms with Rocky Steel since the snake incident. He's quite a laugh apparently. I'm sure she'd ask him about Joe if you wanted her to. No guarantees of course, but there's always a chance he'd say yes. And if he did, it would all be above board and official."

Ellie looked at Sophie. "I don't know...I just hadn't thought about interviewing a boy...but a boy might be *more* interesting for the readers," she said with a grin. "Especially if he's as attractive as Claire says!"

A bubble of excitement rose up inside Ellie. It *was* a good thought. Maybe it wouldn't happen, but she ought to try. She was really grateful for Sophie's help. "Okay!" she said. "Let's give it a try. But I'd like to tell Francesca before we ask Claire. I told her I'd be trying to interview a girl, so I ought to warn her that it might be a boy instead."

"That's sensible," said Sophie. "Go on then. Why don't you ask her right now? I'm getting all excited about it, and I'm not even involved!"

Ellie screwed up her sandwich bag and threw it in the bin. "I will! Thanks, Sophie!"

Francesca hardly ever took lunch out, and when Ellie arrived back in the office she was still at her desk, working. An untouched sandwich and a tub of yoghurt sat next to her keyboard. There was no sign of Piano, or Debbie, on reception. Francesca was scrupulous at urging her staff to get away from the office for a little while every day, but she seldom took her own advice.

She raised her head as Ellie reached her desk and smiled. "You're back early."

"Yes." Ellie shuffled her feet. "I wanted to talk to you about the idea I had to interview the daughter of a celebrity."

Francesca looked sympathetic. "Have you drawn a blank? I did warn you. But well done for trying."

"The thing is..." Ellie paused. "Do you know the band Steel Vortex?"

Francesca unwrapped her sandwich. "Ye-es?"

"Well apparently the lead singer is staying at the Europa, with his son, and I wondered if I might try to interview him. The son, I mean. I know I said it would be a girl, but you were right. I couldn't get anyone to agree."

Francesca nodded slowly. "Well...some of our readers are certainly into heavy metal. But what makes you think it would be any easier to get an interview with a boy?"

"I don't...or at least, there's no reason why it should be, but...at least I know he's in town."

"Interviewing the son could be an interesting angle. How old is he?"

"Fifteen, and very good-looking apparently."

Francesca smiled. "Can I ask who your source is?"

Ellie explained about Sophie's friend, and Francesca smiled with approval. "Sophie's friend sounds like a good person to know. But she won't get into trouble if you use this information, will she? The hotel will almost certainly take the view that staff ought to protect their guests' anonymity."

Ellie thought about it. "I suppose you might be right if it was any other celebrity," she said. "But Sophie says that Claire would be happy to ask Rocky Steel herself, as she gets on with him so well. If he agrees that his son could be interviewed it would be official. If he says no, well that'll be the end of it I suppose." She tried to wait while Francesca took a small bite out of her sandwich and chewed it thoughtfully, but she had to add something.

"Sophie said that Claire gets on so well with Rocky because his snake made her have a panic attack and he's been teasing her about it ever since."

A smile passed over Francesca's face and she put her hand up to cover her mouth.

"I said I couldn't do anything though, until I'd spoken to you first."

Francesca finished her mouthful and smiled. "Very wise. Thank you for doing that." She peeled the top off her yoghurt. "I don't see any harm in Sophie's friend asking, if she's happy. If the answer is yes perhaps you could get the phone number and I'll make the arrangements."

Ellie couldn't stop grinning. "Thanks, Francesca! Fingers crossed."

"Indeed," said Francesca. "Fingers crossed. But don't get so carried away with all this that you forget about Ferdinand's afternoon walk, will you?"

"Of course not," said Ellie. "Or the coffee run this afternoon. I'll make sure I do both.

Excuse me...I'll just go and tell Sophie the good news!"

Ellie couldn't bear to wait for the lift. Instead, she skipped down the three flights of stairs and down again into the basement, where Sophie worked. But there was no sign of Sophie, or her post cart. She was probably making some deliveries. Ellie waited for a few minutes, hoping she'd turn up, but in the end she left a note. She knew Sophie wouldn't have her phone on if she was delivering, and Ellie was afraid that she might forget to switch it back on afterwards. She was just reluctantly leaving the post room when her friend reappeared.

"Hello?" said Sophie in surprise. "Do you have an answer already?"

"Yes!" said Ellie. "Where were you? I came down and you weren't here."

Sophie laughed. "I don't *live* here," she said. "I am allowed out occasionally you know!

Actually I was taking a load of cardboard outside for recycling. And there was so much I had to use my trolley. Come on then. What did she say?"

Ellie told Sophie what Francesca had said, and Sophie looked very pleased. "Hang on then," she said abandoning her trolley. "I'll give Claire a ring."

Ellie waited impatiently for Claire to answer. Then Sophie spoke for a few moments and put the phone down. "Claire's busy with someone. She'll call back when she has a minute."

Ellie was crestfallen, but tried not to show it. "Thanks, Sophie. It's really kind of you to do this."

"Well I might only be the post girl, and not the editor," she said. "But *Heart* is my magazine too, and you're my friend. Why wouldn't I want to help you get a scoop?"

Ellie hung around chatting for a while, but soon lunchtime was over, Claire hadn't rung back, and she knew she really ought to be at her desk.

"I'll ring you as soon as I hear anything," said Sophie. "Don't worry. Just hope for the best."

"I will!" said Ellie.

Back upstairs, Piano had returned, clutching a collection of bags from several shops. She was showing Debbie a lovely silky top, but she shoved it back in the bag as Ellie came in. *Be unfriendly then!* thought Ellie. She knew better than to expect anything else from Piano. Still, she couldn't squash the tinge of hurt that welled up as she passed.

For the first part of the afternoon, Ellie worked steadily through her list of pop stars, actresses and the like, trying to find the next person to interview. Most of the megastars were out of town for the summer, but one agent did promise to ring back about his client, a singer who'd won an MTV award last year and was making a new album.

Then it was time for the coffee run, and after that, she had to take Ferdinand for his walk. It was actually something of a relief to get out. She was finding it hard to sit still and wait for a call. Ellie did realize that Claire would be busy, and that maybe Rocky wouldn't even be in the hotel for most of the day, but it was hard to remain patient. How could she bear it if she had to wait until tomorrow? She was trying not to hope too much, but now she'd got used to the idea of interviewing Joe Steel she really, really wanted to.

"Come on, Ferdi," she said, when he'd stopped running about and had begun sniffing around his favourite trees. "Let's go back if you've had enough exercise."

She looked hard in Francesca's direction as she returned Ferdinand to his basket in the Editor in Chief's office, but Francesca was on the phone, with her back to the door. Ellie took off Ferdinand's lead, and hung it up. Angel was sitting at her huge desk, looking as immaculate as a model on a shoot, as she always did. She glanced up as Ellie made for the door. "I hope you get some useful information tomorrow. Don't forget to sort out what you want to ask beforehand. You can never be too well prepared."

Ellie hesitated, but it was apparent that Angel didn't want to have a conversation.

"Off you go then."

Ellie went, being careful to close the door behind her, but her hand was shaking. Had it all come right, or was Angel referring to some job she'd lined up for Ellie that she knew nothing about yet? She wouldn't put it past the Editor, but no way could she ask. Instead, she went straight to Francesca, but she didn't need to say anything.

"It's all set up," said Francesca with a pleased smile. "Sophie rang up with the information just after you went out, and when I phoned I got through to Rocky himself. He thinks it's a great idea. So, eleven o'clock at his hotel. You can use the library, which is just off the main public area. I've arranged for some drinks and nibbles to be there, and we'll send you in a car. Well done. And perhaps you'd like to nip down to see Sophie and thank her and her friend too."

"That's brilliant!" said Ellie. "I'll go and see her straight away!"

As she passed Piano's desk, the older girl gave her a poisonous look. Once again, Ellie was on her way to getting a brilliant article for *Heart*, and Piano was left feeling jealous. Ellie knew it wasn't charitable, but with the way Piano treated her, she just didn't care. Instead she shot Piano a triumphant look as she strode confidently out of the room.

Down in the post room she gave Sophie a big hug. "Please thank Claire for me. I was afraid I wouldn't hear until tomorrow and if that had been the case I'd have simply *died*!"

Sophie laughed. "Claire was run off her feet earlier, and Rocky was in his room, but he came down to speak to some journalists and she caught him then. Apparently he's been hounded by the press outside the hotel today. They want to hear the latest on his divorce."

"Oh dear," said Ellie. "I didn't realize he was getting divorced. Poor Joe."

"Sad, isn't it?" said Sophie. "But you know what some of the papers are like. They almost prefer celebrity divorces to celebrity weddings."

"I suppose," said Ellie. "Oh Sophie!" she said, unable to feel anything but excitement. "It's been such an up and down day, but thanks to you, tomorrow is going to be *brilliant*!"

Joe Steel

The next morning, Ellie could hardly bear to wait until eleven o'clock. She had decided to dress down a little for the interview. She didn't have anything terribly grungy, but she did her best with a denim skirt and some heavily made-up eyes. Her mum, who didn't usually approve of too much make-up, frowned but said nothing.

Ellie wished Hannah had been around. She'd have loved to ask her advice, and maybe borrow the scruffy old leather jacket Hannah had inherited when her older sister had gone to university. But Hannah was still on holiday, and still not communicating, so it was no good wishing for the impossible. Besides, Angel's high expectations for the dress code of her staff meant that anything too grungy would almost certainly be vetoed. It didn't matter how scruffy the guests chose to be, the staff of *Heart* should always be impeccably turned out. And anyway, if Claire was right, the son of Rocky Steel was probably totally unlike his spectacularly untidy father.

Ellie had done loads of background research for the interview. But what she hadn't managed to find was a good photograph of Joe. In all the pictures he either had his back to the camera, or had dark glasses on, with his long hair falling over his face. It was impossible to make out what he really looked like.

She'd done the first coffee run and had taken Ferdinand out for a brief trot around the park. Now she was back sitting at her desk, waiting for the car to arrive to take her the short distance to the hotel. *Would talking to him be just like chatting to the boys at school?* she wondered. *Or would he be totally rock and roll? And would he sound very American?* From the research she'd done she knew that he was English, but had spent a lot of time in the USA, since his parents had gone to live there some years earlier.

When the main reception desk downstairs rang through to say that the car had arrived, Ellie jumped to her feet and grabbed her bag. She double-checked that she had her notebook and pen and made her way to the door.

"Good luck," called Francesca, and Ellie turned to thank her before hurrying to the lift. In spite of being rather nervous, Ellie was confident that she could handle the whole thing without any problems. It would be up to her to put Joe at his ease, so she must be friendly but professional.

It didn't take long to get to the hotel, which looked very grand. There was even a doorman.

He opened the door for her, and smiled. Ellie didn't think she looked lost, but he seemed to think she might be.

"Reception is straight through here," he said cheerily. "They will help with whatever you need."

"Thank you," said Ellie.

The hotel lobby was enormous, and the thick carpet muffled every sound so effectively it made her want to whisper. She waited at the desk for a couple of minutes, while the receptionist attended to a large woman with several pieces of luggage. Once the woman had gone, with a young porter to help her with her luggage, the receptionist looked at his computer screen for a few seconds and then smiled at Ellie.

"Can I help you?"

"I'm from *Heart* magazine," said Ellie, feeling rather important. "I'm here to do an interview with Joe Steel."

The receptionist tapped a few computer keys. "And your name is…?"

"Ellie Ixos," said Ellie.

"Ah yes. I have you here. We're expecting you. You'll be in the library…" He pointed to one side. "It's not really a separate room, but it's tucked away, and will suit you fine, I think. I'll ring up and let them know you're here."

"Thank you."

Ellie made her way to the book-lined corner that was the hotel library. It was perfect. There were a couple of comfortable chairs and a low table, piled with magazines. As she was deciding which chair to sit on, a waitress arrived with a tray full of drinks and tempting nibbles, which she set out on the table. *Heart* magazine, or at least Francesca, had thought of everything.

Ellie sat down and opened her notebook, but before she had time to read over the questions she proposed asking Joe, he arrived.

The tall, slim figure hesitated for only a second before striding into the library. He looked a couple of years older than Ellie, was wearing scruffy, low-slung jeans, and a rather crumpled T-shirt. In some respects he could have been any one of the many ordinary boys she passed in the street every day, but Ellie was sure she detected in him a confidence that set him apart. Not many teenage boys would be so self-assured in these surroundings, unless they were used to them. She quickly scribbled *confident* in her notebook before getting up to greet him.

Ellie didn't usually approach boys she hadn't met before with such ease, but she was in charge here, and she didn't want to appear nervous. It was her interview, and whatever happened was up to her. So she crossed the floor quickly and held out her hand with a smile. "Hi! I'm Ellie Ixos."

Joe looked at her hand and she withdrew it

awkwardly. Maybe he was right. People of their age didn't shake hands as a rule. That was something older people usually did.

"Hi." Joe shook his long, dark brown fringe out of his eyes. He looked amused, and smiled slightly. Ellie's heart did a little flip. She hadn't thought that he was her type, but he *was* rather good-looking. There was definitely something about him.

"So...have a seat." Ellie retreated to her chair and he collapsed nonchalantly into his, carelessly sprawling his long limbs.

"There are some weird book titles here," he said before she could frame her first question. "I noticed one the other day called *Avoiding Huge Ships*. Who's going to want to read that?" His transatlantic drawl made him even more appealing to Ellie.

She replied quickly. "Sailors, I suppose?" and almost immediately regretted her words. Judging by his expression he hadn't meant it seriously. But it seemed he was willing to try conversation again.

"All we can see from our hotel suite is the garden," he volunteered in a disgusted voice. "I was hoping for a view of that huge wheel you have by the river, or maybe the Tower of London. Who wants to see a garden in London? And they charge extra for that. It's crazy!"

"Oh." Ellie was rather thrown, but tried to be helpful. "Well," she considered. "I suppose whoever booked the suite could have asked if there was a good view."

"Coulda," he agreed. "Shoulda..." He shrugged. "But didn't." He smiled at her, and Ellie found herself smiling back.

Joe leaned back in his chair and looked at the nibbles on the side table. "Am I allowed some of those?"

"Of course!" Ellie was surprised that he had even asked, though Claire had said he was polite. And it *had* been polite of him to ask, but now, after reaching for the nuts he was tossing them haphazardly into his mouth, and paying no attention when several missed and rolled onto the floor. *Typical boy*, thought Ellie.

"Didn't have time for breakfast," he offered, although she hadn't asked why he seemed so hungry.

"So, Joe..."

He looked at her and she tried to arrange her face into one of professional interest, though what she really wanted to do was grin at him. "What's it like having Rocky Steel for a dad?"

"Well..." Joe began to look a bit shifty. "It's all right, I suppose. He's quite kind...and he can be really generous. He buys us...me...stuff when we're on tour."

"What sort of stuff?"

Joe shrugged. "Just...stuff. You know... games...books...to keep us occupied."

"Do you get to go to all his gigs?"

Joe shrugged, and another couple of nuts rolled off his lap and onto the floor. "Some of them."

"That must be very exciting. Because he does do outrageous things onstage, doesn't he?"

Joe looked rather embarrassed. Ellie supposed it could be embarrassing having a father who in her opinion wore ridiculous clothes, and rode his motorbike onstage, but that's what the readers would want to know. Did Joe have ambitions to be as crazy as his father, or not? It was difficult to tell much from the boy sitting opposite her. And now he didn't seem quite as confident as she had at first thought.

"Didn't your dad fall off the stage on his motorbike one night?"

"Did he?" Joe looked confused, but he rapidly recovered himself. "Oh yeah, p'raps he did. I guess. Last year some time, wasn't it?"

"You'd forgotten?" Ellie was astonished.

"But I'm sure I read somewhere that his leg was in plaster for ages and the band were getting worried that it might not mend properly."

"Oh? Right. I mean yeah. That's it. It was worrying at the time. Can I have some of that soda?"

Before she could answer, or pour it for him, Joe had leaped up and slopped some into a glass. It foamed up and overflowed into the tray the glasses were on.

"Oops."

"It doesn't matter." Ellie got up too and helped him mop up the spill with a couple of napkins. Their hands touched and they both pulled away. "So do you mind having a dad who does things like that?"

Joe looked at her, and Ellie looked earnestly back at him, with her most empathetic interviewer expression this time securely in place. To her disappointment, instead of opening up, he turned away and swigged the drink in one. Then he went over to one of the bookshelves and stared at the books, saying nothing.

Ellie was worried. This wasn't going at all well. She couldn't seem to find anything that would make him open up. The trouble was, every time she looked at him she couldn't help thinking how attractive he was. Did that get in the way of her being a professional interviewer? Maybe she was putting him off because he thought she was flirting with him, but she really, truly wasn't.

She wished Francesca was there. Francesca would have known how to gain Joe's trust and get him to start talking. She wanted the real deal on Joe's life, not this surface stuff where he said nothing of any consequence. But how could she get through to him? Should she say she was sorry to hear about his parents' divorce? Would that help, or make things worse? The questions flew through her mind, but she didn't have any answers. She simply didn't have enough experience of interviews to know if she was playing this right or making some silly mistake. Ellie wondered if she ought to make an excuse and go, but she didn't want to admit defeat.

She told herself that she ought to give it another try. He hadn't had any crisps yet, and he'd been enthusiastic about the snacks. In fact that was almost all he *had* been enthusiastic about, apart from maybe the books. Perhaps she could lure him back to the chair with crisps. Or should she take them to him and share the book titles with him for a while? Would that help? Did he really like books? Or was he just bored with the interview and her?

Ellie picked up the dish of crisps. She had to do something. She could hardly build an article around Joe having a possible interest in books! Fleetingly, she wondered if she ought to try matching his silence. She'd heard that loads of people got unnerved by silences, and had to fill them. But she rejected that idea. It would be unnerving for her, but might not be for him. That would never do!

She looked at the bowl of crisps in her hand. She wouldn't take them over to the window. She didn't feel right conducting an interview standing up. If he wanted more to eat he'd have to come back and sit down. Then she'd give it one last go. But as she cleared her throat to speak, Joe Steel spun round and glared at her.

"It's no good!" he said angrily. "I can't do this."

Unmasked

Ellie looked at Joe in horror. "What do you mean?" It was one thing for her to consider pulling out of the interview, but quite another if he thought she wasn't worth talking to.

"Yeah, well. It's not easy pretending to be someone else."

Ellie stared at the frowning boy in front of her. "I don't know what you're talking about," she said at last. "Do you mean you're trying to behave like your father but don't really want to? Actually, I was going to ask if you felt very different from your dad."

Now it was his turn to stare at her. "No!" he said, taking a handful of the crisps she was holding and throwing himself back into his chair. "No way!"

Ellie sat down and waited until he'd chomped the crisps and brushed the worst of the crumbs from his T-shirt. "Well what *do* you mean?"

Joe Steel was having difficulty meeting Ellie's eyes. "I feel kinda bad."

"You don't need to feel bad," said Ellie, sympathetically. "It can't be easy."

He looked at her now, and the smile was back, reaching his eyes as well as his mouth. "You're really great, you know that? I thought you'd be some old lady journalist, but you're my sort of age. That was a real shock. That's why I can't do this. It's not fair."

Ellie couldn't help smiling back at him, but she was even more confused than before. "I still don't understand what the problem is," she said. "All I wanted to do was ask you a few questions about what life is like, spending the summer touring around with your dad."

"That's just it," he said. "I'm not spending the summer with my dad." He must have seen the confusion in her expression because he leaned forward until he was looking right into her face. "Rocky Steel isn't my dad."

Ellie was thrown into turmoil. If Rocky wasn't Joe's real father, who was? And what did that do to the interview? She wished she'd done more research. How long had Joe's mum and Rocky been together? Had Joe only recently become the stepson of a rock star? If so, surely the whole interview was pointless? She had to try and rescue something out of this mess. Then another thought struck her. Could this be something to do with the divorce? Had it just come out that Joe wasn't really Rocky's son?

Ellie didn't really want to say anything about that sorry mess, but she had to do something, so she looked at him sympathetically. "So he's actually your stepfather?"

Joe was shaking his head.

"No! No! I'm trying to explain but you just don't get it. Rocky Steel isn't my dad...because I'm not Joe."

Ellie fumbled to put the bowl of crisps onto the table without dropping them. "You're not Joe Steel?" she said faintly.

"No." The boy studied his shoes. "I'm not... Sorry."

Ellie was reeling from this piece of information, but she tried to remain calm. "Then who are you?" she asked at last.

"I'm Connor."

"Connor who?"

"Constantis...but you won't have heard of me."

"You're right. I haven't." The thought struck Ellie that she had jumped to conclusions when he...Connor had appeared. Had she asked him who he was? No, she didn't think she had. She'd simply introduced herself, and assumed that he was the boy she'd been expecting. It must all be her fault...but then...surely any normal person would have put her right straight away? Why hadn't he? Ellie's embarrassment quickly turned to annoyance. How dare this... *person* come strolling in here, impersonating Joe Steel. How had he managed it? He'd seemed *nice*, but maybe he wasn't as nice as she'd thought. He'd been taking advantage of her. He'd been eating *Heart*'s nibbles, and drinking their cola and...how *dare* he? Ellie glared at him. She felt humiliated. Had she been set up? If so, by whom? She was sure it wasn't the sort of thing Sophie would do... surely her friend Claire wouldn't either? And Francesca had arranged the interview in good faith. So it must be something to do with this boy who had suddenly become Connor instead of Joe. But how? And why?

"Does that mean I can't have any more potato chips?"

He was smiling hesitantly at her, but she wasn't in the mood to be won over. She folded her arms, leaned back in her chair and glared even harder at him. "You'd better explain what you think you're doing here."

He put his hands up, as if in surrender. "I will," he said. "But wait a minute. How about another drink?"

Before she could reply he'd leaped out of his chair and poured himself more cola, without spilling it this time. He poured one for her too, and gave it to her before he sat back down.

"Okay. Confession time." He paused, put his glass on the table and took a deep breath. "Well, I'm at the same high school as Joe. We've been friends since for ever. You see, most times when his dad goes on tour, Joe stays home with his mom, but this summer she went back to Denmark, to spend the summer with her family. Her own dad isn't well, and Joe knew it would be a heavy summer if he went there. It isn't even as if he knows the Danish relatives, and being stuck in the country didn't appeal, so his dad said he could go on tour with him."

Ellie thought she could see where this was heading, but she asked anyway.

"So Joe asked if you wanted to go as well?"

"Right. And it was the most fun to begin with. We went to a few gigs, ate lots of food, chilled out. You know the sort of thing."

Ellie nodded, although she'd never been on any sort of tour in her life she could imagine it.

"But now I guess it's got a bit boring."

"Really?"

Connor frowned. "It's not that I wasn't pleased to be asked. Joe's my buddy, and the rest of the kids at school were sooo jealous. But we've been jetting all over the place, to some countries I've always wanted to visit, but once we were there we were mostly stuck in hotels and didn't get to see anything, or go anywhere.

I want to see stuff! I haven't even been on the London Eye yet and it's only over there somewhere!" Connor waved his hand vaguely towards the hotel entrance. "But Joe's gone all celebrity, even though he *isn't*. He's no fun to be with. He skulks around indoors in his dark glasses as if he's being hounded by the press. But he's *not*." Connor looked exasperated. "I feel like a minder...one that's locked up with the person he's minding." He paused, and Ellie could see a smile fighting for space on his grumpy face. "It's stupid," he said at last, his smile winning.

"What about his dad though?" said Ellie. "Doesn't he want Joe to see something of the places you're going? It's a great opportunity, isn't it?"

Connor sighed. "Money's no object," he said. "But time is. Joe's dad is busy, and I'm sure he thinks that because Joe has me around, everything is fine. He said we could go where we like as long as we're together, but Joe won't go to places I want to, and..." Connor paused. "The other day he gave me the slip, and I didn't know *where* he was. His dad would have gone *mental* if he'd known about that. Joe's dad never stops working. He doesn't have time to sort us out. It might not look like it, but he works really hard. Even all this stuff about the divorce."

"How is that work?" said Ellie scathingly.

Connor smiled at her. "It's all promotion for his latest album. The media asked the question about divorce because Astrid, Joe's mom has been away. So his mom and dad have been going along with it, to keep his dad in the press. The more he's in the news, the more albums he sells. See?"

Connor sat back, looking impressed at the Steels' savvy. "It's amazing. Joe's dad's been out there this morning, looking even more out of it than usual, giving the impression that he's trying to pretend nothing is wrong with his marriage when it is." He grinned at Ellie. "But of course there isn't *really* anything wrong with their marriage! Pretty clever, eh? It's a sort of double bluff. You have to admire it."

Ellie wasn't convinced, and didn't smile back. "You haven't told me yet why you ended up coming over here to do Joe's interview. Isn't it a sort of fraud or something, doing that?"

Connor shook his head. "No way! It wasn't supposed to be that heavy a deal."

"How heavy a deal *was* it supposed to be?" said Ellie cynically.

Connor bit his lip. "It was because Joe didn't want to be interviewed."

Now Ellie was astonished. "Didn't want to be interviewed for *Heart*?"

"Well don't blame me!" Connor sounded totally fed up. "It's not my fault!"

"Well it's certainly not mine," said Ellie primly.

They seemed to have reached stalemate.

Ellie was wondering frantically what she was going to say to Francesca. Piano would so enjoy making a big deal of how gullible Ellie had been. It was going to be *awful*. It really stung that the interview idea should have gone so badly wrong. None of it had been her fault, but she had been totally humiliated.

"The thing is..." Connor appeared contrite. "I'm sorry. I was just trying to help out a friend. His dad would have gone ballistic if he'd known Joe was going to dip out."

"So why did he?"

Connor sighed. "He doesn't want to do many things that his dad wants him to do." There was a pause. "His dad wants him to appear onstage with him, but he keeps refusing. And last night he persuaded me to come to this interview instead of him. He said it wouldn't matter. Not many people know what he looks like because he always keeps his head down, and his hair over his eyes....*and* he wears dark glasses as well. He reckoned I could easily be mistaken for him." Connor looked earnestly at Ellie. "He said it would be a laugh if I did it, and that I could tell you what you wanted to know. But it wasn't easy..." His voice trailed off and he looked away.

"So why did he agree in the first place if he didn't want to be interviewed?"

"His dad didn't even bother to *ask* him. It was Rocky who agreed, not Joe. And the thing is...the time Joe disappeared I was so freaked that he wouldn't be back before his dad. I tell you, you don't want to get on the wrong side of Joe's dad. Besides, I was left in the hotel feeling like his anxious mom or something."

"So where had Joe gone?" asked Ellie.

"I don't know. He was mooching around the streets I guess, but he wouldn't tell me anything about it. Just that he needed to get away for a bit."

"Well, that's understandable, isn't it?" said Ellie. "If his dad is putting pressure on him."

"I guess so," said Connor slowly.

"Well," Ellie couldn't help feeling for Connor, but she was still angry with him, "between the two of you, you've really dropped me in it. I'm supposed to be getting material for an article, but the right person isn't here. How am I going to explain that? I'm going to look so stupid."

The truth of what she was saying hit Ellie hard, and to her horror, hot tears of self-pity began to spill from her eyes. Now she was feeling more humiliated than she'd ever felt in her whole life. How was she ever going to recover from this morning of utter disaster?

8

Rescue plan

Ellie was trying desperately to compose herself, and Connor was looking at her in horror.

"Oh no, please don't cry."

"I'm not crying," she said, furiously rubbing the tears from her cheeks. "I only cry about important things like war and...and animals that have been injured."

"Oh. Sorry. Well if it's any help I cried at the film *I, Robot*."

She wondered if he was laughing at her, but it appeared not.

"Anyway," she said, sounding more forceful than she meant to. "I ought to go." She got up and he did too, looking anxious.

"But what about the interview? What are you going to say to cover your back?"

Ellie swigged her drink and the sugar rush made her feel stronger. "I'll think of something, I expect." She picked up the empty nut dish and put it on the tray. He took the crisp bowl and offered it to her. She looked at the few crumbs left and gave him a slight smile. "You might as well eat them, I suppose. Otherwise they'll only get thrown away."

But Connor was concentrating on Ellie's problem. "Why not tell them that you haven't got enough for an article yet?"

She looked at him curiously. "Why wouldn't I have enough? And anyway, how would that help?"

He scratched his head. "Well, maybe I…Joe got called away and you couldn't finish the interview, so you are going to have to give it another shot."

"Ye-es. Maybe. I suppose. But then what?"

Connor put the crisps down and pulled out his phone. "Give me your number. I'll try to get Joe to meet you. Honestly. I will." He hesitated. "If I possibly can."

"But what if he still refuses? What then?" Ellie was having trouble thinking straight.

Connor jiggled his phone from hand to hand. "Then you tell me your questions and I'll get the answers for you. How about that?"

He looked so desperate to put things right that Ellie believed him, and she had to admit that the idea was rather neat too. "Oka-ay." It couldn't do any harm to give him her number. And maybe he might even come up with the goods for her. He seemed keen enough.

Ellie told Connor her number and he keyed it into his phone. "Here, have mine too," he offered. She tapped in the number and then there didn't seem anything more to say.

"Well," he said after an awkward pause. He gave her a smile, and she felt herself responding.

After all, it was nice of him to try and help her out, even if he had partly caused the problem in the first place.

"I'll see you out. Are you catching a cab?"

"Francesca told me to ask reception to get one for me when I'd finished."

"Okay. So let's do that."

Together they hurried to the reception desk. The man who had been on duty had gone, and his place had been taken by a woman with long blonde hair. She smiled at Connor and Ellie. "Can I help?"

Ellie explained, and the woman nodded. "If you take a seat I'll call for one now. It should only be a few minutes."

"Thanks," said Ellie.

Ellie and Connor were both quiet while they waited for the taxi. There didn't seem to be any more to say. But Ellie found herself taking sideways glances at her companion. She had been angry that her interview was wrecked, but she couldn't help liking Connor, in spite of that.

After a few minutes, the receptionist told them the taxi had arrived. They both got up, and Connor walked Ellie to the door. The doorman held open the door of the taxi, which made her feel pretty special, but before she could get in, Connor spoke.

"Thanks for the eats and soda. And I'm sorry about Joe, but it was good to meet you, Ellie. I'll be in touch." Then, he suddenly reached forward and gave her a hug, and a kiss on her cheek. He dived back through the hotel door and was gone.

In the taxi, Ellie could feel herself blush and was glad he hadn't seen that. But Connor had kissed her! It had come totally out of the blue and had made her heart race. Ellie tried to think. She needed time to sort out what she was going to say once she got back to the office. She didn't want to tell anyone about what had happened, not even Sophie. The only person she would have liked to confide in was Hannah, but there was no point in thinking about that.

Instead, she began to wonder whether she did have the makings of an article. Could she write about what had *really* happened? Then she'd have to admit that she'd been duped of course. But would it be worth reading? No one liked to look a fool, but what if she could laugh at herself? Would it be worth it to get a good piece?

Still running alongside these thoughts was the memory of Connor's sudden and unexpected kiss. What was all that about? He hadn't wanted to shake her hand when they met, but he had given her a hug and a kiss when they parted. He didn't have to do that. He could have just let her go.

Ellie wasn't sure how she felt about it. She'd been very angry with him for a while, but he'd offered to try and put things right, and he *had* just been helping out his mate, which she supposed was pretty okay really. Did she like him? Well…yes, she supposed she did. Or at least, if he proved himself to be genuine by doing his best with Joe she might allow herself to like him.

As she reached the office, Ellie was still feeling a bit vulnerable. She was still smarting, knowing she'd been tricked. But at least Connor had owned up. Ellie shuddered to think what could have happened if he hadn't let on. She might have written and published an article based on a lie. It didn't bear thinking about!

"Ellie! Back already? How did you get on?"

It was Francesca.

"Um…" Ellie concentrated on rummaging in her bag to find her sandwiches for lunch. "Okayish, but I need more really, and we ran out of time."

"Oh?" Francesca looked surprised. Then her expression cleared. "Well, no doubt he leads a busy life. Did you make another date?"

"Not exactly," said Ellie. "He's going to get back to me."

"Fair enough," said Francesca. She thought for a moment. "You know, occasionally I think there's going to be an article in something, but for one reason or another it just doesn't work out."

Ellie looked at her. "Really?"

Francesca nodded. "Really. Your original idea was excellent though, and if you do get what you need from young Joe Steel I'm sure there's a good piece there waiting to be written."

She smiled, and suddenly Ellie felt a whole lot better. Francesca wasn't at all suspicious about Ellie's lack of copy, and if Connor could come up with the answers she wanted she'd be sorted. "Is it okay if I go for an early lunch?" she said. "I could take Ferdinand at the same time and go to the park. It's a really nice day."

"Okay," said Francesca. "Why don't you? Angel has a whole load of clothes for you to unpack, but you can do that this afternoon."

Ellie glanced at Piano on her way to collect Ferdinand, but Piano didn't make any remarks about the interview, Joe, or anything else. In fact she totally ignored Ellie, and kept on working. Ellie had the feeling that she'd got away with it. Unless she chose to write about being temporarily duped, no one would ever know.

By the end of the day, Ellie was on top of the world. She'd had great fun unpacking the clothes. Angel was going to profile a new, young designer and almost her whole collection had been delivered so Angel could choose which clothes to photograph and feature in *Heart*. Ellie absolutely loved the funky dresses, cool tops, and especially the new jeans. Angel wanted to know what she thought, and Ellie hoped Angel might put some of Ellie's thoughts in her article. The collection had been sold to one of Ellie's favourite fashion stores, and already Ellie was planning what she would buy for herself when they became available. But then, Angel had suggested Ellie take a couple of things from the collection to wear, and test her friends' reactions. It was an amazing way to end the day, and Ellie went for her bus with a designer carrier bag in her hand and a big smile on her face. With Angel, you never quite knew what might happen next, but her offer had totally raised Ellie's mood. She couldn't wait to show off her new top and jeans to her friends. She could just imagine their squeals of excitement as they realized that they were getting a sneak preview of new designs that hadn't made it onto the high street yet.

9

Connor needs help

That evening, while Ellie was getting ready for bed, her phone buzzed. As soon as she heard the sound she couldn't help herself, and her heart leaped, hoping it was a message from Hannah. She leaned over and grabbed the phone, but the text was from another friend, Naomi. *Weekend starts here! Coffee tomorrow. Usual place. Bex's birthday. 11.00.*

Ellie hadn't forgotten about Bex's birthday. In fact she had a sweet little purse all ready to give her. It would be good to see some of her school friends too, so she texted back straight away. *I'll be there!* Then she put the phone down, and climbed into bed with her father's notebook in her hand. Ellie had made a couple of notes during the interview with Connor, before she'd known that he wasn't Joe Steel. Francesca had suggested that Ellie should think about it over the weekend, to see if she could make do with what she'd got, or if she really needed more. Ellie already knew she didn't have anything like enough information for an article, but based on what Connor had told her about him Ellie had decided to rough out a few really good questions to ask the real Joe. Before she could find the right page her phone buzzed again. The message wasn't from any of her school friends, or from Hannah. It was from Connor.

Can you get into town tomorrow morning 11.00ish?

Ellie read the text several times. She wasn't sure how to respond. Had Connor persuaded Joe to meet her? She hoped so, but he hadn't made it very clear. And he'd suggested the same time as Bex's birthday get-together. That was annoying. But maybe she could combine the two? Then she could give Bex her present, see her friends, and meet Connor and possibly Joe too, all at the same time. They could always stay on after everyone else had left, so she could ask her questions. Ellie grinned. It would be fun to have a boy, or even two, in tow that no one else knew. Her friends would be intrigued, maybe even impressed! Yes! It would be a winner on so many levels. Her phone would be buzzing after everyone had met them. They'd all want to know who the boys were, and how she'd met them, but she wouldn't tell until Connor and Joe had left the city. And she had her cool new clothes to wear too. Saturday morning was going to be fun!

Before she could change her mind, Ellie texted Connor, telling him that she'd meet him in town. She told him the name of the café, which wasn't too far from the hotel, and hoped he'd agree to meet there. She didn't tell him that her friends would be around. That might put him off. She sent the text and then lay back with her hands behind her head, waiting. After a few seconds he texted back to say that he'd be there.

Ellie put the phone away and settled down to sleep with a smile on her face. Tomorrow would be great. Let Connor think that he and Joe were just meeting her. He'd tricked her. Why shouldn't she trick him a little? Except it wouldn't really be a trick. He hadn't said they wanted to meet her alone, and she hadn't said she wouldn't be. She remembered the way he'd hurriedly kissed her, and her smile widened. Of course she wanted to get enough information about Joe for a good article, but there was no reason why she shouldn't enjoy herself as well. Ellie was looking forward to meeting Joe, but she was also looking forward to seeing Connor again. In fact she was looking forward to it very much indeed.

10
Boy missing

On Saturday morning, Ellie rolled out of bed determined to make a splash at the café in town. It wasn't just her friends who hung out there. Lots of people did. It was a cool place to be seen, and today she had her new jeans and top to show off, as well as the two boys, who she hoped would turn up. She took special care over her make-up, ate a piece of toast, grabbed her bag and left the flat, banging the door behind her.

She was in good time to catch the bus, and it wasn't too long before she was there. The whole area was buzzing with people enjoying their weekend, but Ellie saw Naomi almost straight away. She had managed to bag their usual table in the window of the café, and was waving wildly at Ellie through the glass. Ellie went in, queued to buy a drink and took it over to the table.

"Cool top!" Naomi said at once. "I don't think I've seen it before. And are those new jeans?"

Ellie put her drink down and grinned at Naomi. "They're from a new designer...so new they're not in the shops yet!"

"No! Really? Wow!" She stood up to give Ellie a hug, and nearly knocked her drink over. "I suppose you got them from *Heart*?"

Ellie nodded.

"I'm sooo jealous," said Naomi. "Go on, turn round so I can see them properly."

Ellie twirled around and then sat down with a giggle.

"Wait till everyone else gets here," said Naomi with a grin. "They'll want to know all the details!"

It wasn't many minutes before most of the other girls arrived. Soon there was a whole gaggle of them, squealing their admiration for Ellie's new clothes.

"I only got them because Angel had finished with them," said Ellie. "And the deal is that I come back with some reactions from you lot."

"Does that mean we might get our comments in the mag?" said Alice.

"I suppose it might," said Ellie.

"Okay. So write this down," said Alice. "Love the new cut of the jeans, and the detail on the pockets."

Ellie scribbled the comment in her notebook. Then Bex, the birthday girl, arrived and Ellie's clothes were forgotten in the crush, as everyone went to hug Bex and give her cards and presents. They all watched as she undid one small parcel after another. Soon the table was a sea of coloured paper and envelopes. Ellie and the others helped clear away the rubbish, making room to admire the make-up, coloured pens and chocolates that people had given Bex.

"I like your top," said Bex to Ellie after the presents had been discussed. "The colours really suit you."

"Thanks," said Ellie, but she wasn't allowed to say any more because Naomi butted in with a grin.

"You won't believe how grand our Ellie has got," she said. "She's now wearing designer clothes before they're in the shops!"

Ellie laughed. "They're going to be in a fashion store," she said. "They'll be everywhere so they're not exclusive designer."

"Well *someone* had to design them," said Naomi firmly.

Ellie got out her notebook and pen again, and scribbled busily until everyone had had their say. By the time she was able to put her pen back in her bag, Ellie was sure Angel would be impressed with all her friends' comments.

And Ellie was enjoying herself so much that for the moment she had forgotten all about Connor and Joe, so she was a bit startled when, all of a sudden, Connor appeared. The girls were looking at him a bit strangely as he stood there, trying to attract Ellie's attention. "Oh, hi, Connor!" said Ellie, getting up and looking vainly for any evidence that he'd managed to bring Joe with him. "Are you on your own then?"

"I guess," he said. "Sorry."

"Are you American?" asked Alice.

Connor nodded.

"Whereabouts are you from?" said Naomi.

"California," said Connor shortly.

"Wow!" said Alice. "That's a cool place to come from."

Ellie could see that Connor didn't seem very comfortable surrounded by her friends, but she didn't feel too bad about it. After all, with no Joe, it seemed her article was still a forlorn hope. Maybe he deserved to suffer a bit as penance for letting her down. In any case, her friends weren't horrible, and she knew they'd soon put him at his ease.

But Connor didn't seem at all happy, and kept shooting agonized glances her way. It seemed obvious that he wanted to speak to her alone, but Ellie wasn't about to desert her friends. Surely he could wait until they left? Naomi and Alice were talking about going shopping, and Bex, along with best friend Fi, was going to meet up with her parents for lunch and a West-End show.

"Are you coming shopping with us?" said Naomi to Ellie, as Bex and Fi left the café.

"Not this time," said Ellie, glancing at Connor. "I've just saved up enough for my mum's birthday, and if I go shopping with you I know I'll spend it all."

"Yeah, right!" said Naomi, nudging Ellie's arm. "We understand."

Eventually the girls all left. Connor slid into the chair opposite Ellie and stared at her. All of a sudden she could see that he looked almost scared.

"What's the matter?" she asked, with a tremor of alarm.

"It's Joe," said Connor. "He's gone."

"Gone?" said Ellie. "You mean he's sloped off again?"

"No," said Connor, and it was obvious how upset he was. "I think he's run away, Ellie. And I'm almost sure he's left the country!"

11
A very strange day

Ellie stared at Connor. "What do you mean, run away? How do you know? And…" She struggled to make sense of the news. "When did he go?"

"I don't know!" said Connor. "I told him about you, and last night he seemed up for meeting, so I sent you that text, but when I woke up this morning, he wasn't there." Ellie could hear desperation in his voice. "Maybe he disturbed me by mistake when he left the room, but something woke me really early. I went to the bathroom, and when I came back I realized he wasn't there."

"You're sure?"

He sounded exasperated. "How many places

do you imagine there are to hide in a hotel suite?"

"Okay. Sorry." Ellie was trying to control the urge to howl. Where did this leave her article? But it looked and sounded as if Connor really was in a state, so she pushed her own feelings to one side. He needed to calm down. "Didn't you tell me that he'd disappeared once before? He came back, didn't he? Surely he will this time too? All you have to do is keep away from the hotel for a bit so his dad thinks you're together. And you can phone him can't you?"

"He's not answering his cellphone," said Connor bleakly. "And the thing is..." He gave a gulp. "I'm scared that this time he's not coming back. His passport was on his night table, but it's not there any more. I reckon he's gone to Italy!"

Ellie felt both horrified and excited at the same time. She didn't want this to become a proper missing person's investigation, of course she didn't, but at the same time it was kind of thrilling. And who knew, there might be an article in it! She pushed that unworthy thought firmly away and concentrated on Connor. He was obviously worried sick. But why on earth would Joe run away to Italy?

"He has an aunt in Italy," Connor explained when she asked. "She lives in Rome. And he's always said how well he gets on with her. But there's this too." He held out a piece of paper, and Ellie took it.

It was part of a sheet of hotel paper, and the only thing scrawled on it in biro was *Colosseum, 25th*. Ellie looked at Connor questioningly, and he hurried to explain.

"It's in Joe's handwriting," he explained. "I googled Colosseum and it's in Rome, Italy. It's a big Roman ruin."

"I think I knew that," said Ellie.

"And the 25th is today," went on Connor.

"I guess that's the clincher. That, and his passport having gone."

"And having an aunt there as well," said Ellie.

Connor nodded. "Yeah."

"So what are you going to do?"

Connor spread his hands. "I don't know! Joe usually stays in bed until nearly lunchtime, so only something he really cared about would get him out of bed so early." He paused, looking more distracted at every moment. "I don't know if I ought to phone the police, or cover for him with his dad or what. And the only person I have to talk to about it is you."

"Well, try not to worry," Ellie said. "Look. Why not have a drink, and we'll talk about what's best to do."

"Okay. You want anything?"

"No thanks. I've already had two."

Ellie watched Connor as he queued for his drink. He was taller than she was, and from the back looked totally grown up. But there was something about his face. A bit of uncertainty, perhaps. He came back, carrying a tray. He was smiling at her, but he was pale, and his smile didn't disguise the worry still carved into his face. Ellie found that she really did want to make that worried expression go away.

"So what do you think has led to this?" she asked as he sat down.

Connor sighed. "That's easy. Rocky wants Joe to join the band as soon as he leaves school. Rocky has some throat trouble, and the band badly needs a new singer. I guess Rocky thinks it would be cool to keep it in the family. Joe made the mistake of singing along with them at a jam session at their house in California a few months ago, and everyone in the band thought he was great. But Joe hates the idea of joining his dad's band." Connor looked at Ellie. "I think Rocky put pressure on him to do this touring thing over the summer, once he realized

Joe didn't want to go to Denmark with his mom, and now we're here, Joe can't bear it. He'd hoped it would be enough if we went to gigs as spectators, but Rocky's always on at him to get up onstage and sing with him."

"Blimey!" Ellie felt grateful that no one had ever tried to make her do something she didn't want to, especially so publicly. That would be *so* embarrassing. "*Can* he really sing?"

Connor nodded. "Oh yeah. We used to do all these school productions, and he had a brilliant voice. He got all the good parts. But since his dad began to pile on the pressure I haven't heard him sing or even listen to music at all."

"It's a shame he agreed to spend the summer with his dad if that's the way he feels," ventured Ellie.

"I said that," agreed Connor, "I said he was stupid...but it was difficult for him. I'm sure he hoped they might sort it all out between them during the tour."

Connor drained his glass, and put it back on the tray. "His dad ought to get off his back. After all, Joe is showing support. He just doesn't want to do the same job as his dad." Connor paused. "I wish Joe had talked to me more. I didn't think it was so bad that he'd run away. And if it was, well, I'm his buddy. He could have spoken to me."

Poor Connor, thought Ellie, *worrying so much about his friend. And poor Joe too. Has he really gone to the Colosseum today? Was he meeting his aunt? Or has Connor got it wrong? Wherever he is. I hope he's all right.*

"So you think Joe's gone to see his aunt to get away from his dad?"

"I guess so." Connor scratched his head. "Maybe he thinks she'll talk to his dad for him. She's his dad's younger sister. But why just go, without telling me?" Connor sounded hurt. "I could have flown back home to the US if he'd told me he was going to do this. But he's left me in the lurch, not knowing what to do. And it's not like him. I suppose that's why I'm so worried. I get to thinking I've figured it out, and then I'm not so sure. If he *hasn't* flown to Italy where *has* he gone?"

"He was supposed to be coming to the café with you?" said Ellie.

Connor shrugged. "He gave me that impression. But maybe he never meant to. Rocky had a gig last night. He probably didn't wake up until after we were supposed to meet you, so Joe must have thought he'd be safe for hours. His dad won't worry if we're both out. He'll assume we're together, like he always does." His mouth twisted bitterly.

"And you've tried his phone?"

"Yeah. No answer. I've left messages of course, and texted."

"Well," Ellie struggled to be helpful. "It does sound as if he's gone abroad. But if he hasn't, where else might he be?"

Connor looked at her. "I have absolutely no idea. The clues about Italy are the only ones we have to go on."

"So when are you going to tell his dad?"

Connor looked scared. "I don't want to tell him at *all*. But I suppose I'll have to eventually." He looked resentful. "I don't have the money to run back home to the US whenever I feel like it. But I tell you, Ellie. That's just what I feel like doing right now."

12
The real Joe Steel

Ellie looked at Connor sympathetically. "Well…" she said. "I don't see why you have to rush back to the hotel to tell Joe's dad right away. If he's gone to Italy there's nothing anyone can do for the moment, and if he hasn't he'll turn up again, won't he?"

"He's pretty streetwise, if that's what you mean," said Connor. "Yeah. He's not stupid. I hope he wouldn't get into trouble, but if he's still in London I suppose he might check into a different hotel for the night if he's not ready to see his dad. That would really drop me in it."

"Well then. He wouldn't do that, would he?"

Connor shot her a wry smile. "I sure hope not."

"So…why not wait a while, and see if he gets in touch. Maybe he's somewhere at the moment where he can't use his phone."

Connor smiled at her. "Could be true," he said. "Like a cinema perhaps. Though it was a bit early for the movies this morning."

"Well, his dad isn't going to worry for hours and hours, is he?" said Ellie. "You've got all day to find out what's going on."

Connor nodded. "A whole day and some of the evening too," he agreed. "Do you wanna hang out with me for a while? It would be much more fun than being on my own all the time."

"Okay," said Ellie. "What do you want to do?"

"Maybe some of those touristy things I haven't got to do yet," said Connor. "How about a bus ride around some of the sights? I've seen those open-topped buses go past sometimes. They sure look fun."

Ellie laughed. "I haven't been on one of those since my cousin came to stay years ago. It rained and we got soaked."

"Well I don't think it's going to rain today," said Connor with the most cheerful smile Ellie had seen on his face so far. "Come on, my treat!"

Ellie hesitated. "Are you sure?"

"Course I am. Most of this trip has been all expenses paid. I've hardly had a chance to spend my own money so, whatever we do today it's on me."

It was a good day for an open-topped bus ride, and Connor did get to see some of the most famous sights. At the same time, they tried to think of places Joe might have gone to if he hadn't flown off to Italy.

"What does Joe like to do?" said Ellie, trying to get inspiration as the bus took them past Buckingham Palace.

"Well, before his dad put him off, he liked to sing," said Connor. "But not heavy rock." He laughed. "Joe's a bit of a romantic. He had a girlfriend back in the States for a while, and he used to sing to her. He told me I should sing too. Choose the right song, with the right lyrics and I'd never be short of a girlfriend. But my voice is terrible." He laughed again. "It would never work for me!"

At the end of the bus ride they mooched along the street for a while, trying to decide what else to do. Connor pulled his phone out of his pocket and sent Joe yet another message and rang him as well, but there was no reply.

"Time is getting on," said Connor, sounding despondent again. "Maybe I should have owned up to Rocky straight away. If something *has* gone wrong he'll never forgive me."

Ellie squeezed his arm sympathetically. "He might have lost his phone," she said. "Or had it stolen." But that led to thoughts of muggings, and she didn't want Connor to start worrying about *that* possibility. She stopped outside a bookshop, and gazed in the window for a moment. Then she saw the very book she'd been meaning to buy for her mum's birthday.

"Do you mind if we go in here?" she said.

Connor shook his head. "Anywhere is good for me. But, Ellie..."

"What is it?"

Connor's mouth twisted. "You're being so great, after I let you down. I just want to say I'm really sorry I didn't get Joe to turn up and talk to you for your article."

Ellie was touched that he'd even remembered, what with Joe's disappearance to think about, and the anger of his father to worry about. "Don't be silly. It's not the end of the world. Not really, not compared to a missing person anyway." Even so, she'd been so close, and she couldn't help regretting it.

They went in and began browsing. Ellie didn't want anything other than the present for her mum, but she loved mooching about in bookshops, and it seemed Connor felt the same way. He wandered over to the sci-fi and fantasy section while she had a look at a new novel by one of her favourite authors on the young adult shelf. Unfortunately, she didn't have enough money to buy it, but she told herself she'd get it next time she was in town.

Ellie took her mum's present to the queue at the counter, and began looking at the notices pinned up on a board by the door while she waited for her turn. There were adverts for a local book group, one card offering Spanish lessons, and another offering salsa dancing classes. There was a poster for a singing workshop and another advertising a cinema club showing foreign language films.

There was something about the notices that was pricking at Ellie's mind. She stared at the board. What was it?

Connor materialized by her side, holding a fat novel with a picture on the cover of a dragon breathing fire, and an unfeasibly muscular man wielding a double-headed axe. Ellie smiled. *"Dragon-slayer of Naxdon. That looks like a hefty read!"*

Connor just smiled.

Ellie's gaze went back to the notices, and then she realized what had niggled at her earlier. "Oh. *Oh!*"

Connor looked amused. "What do you mean? Oh. *Oh?*"

"Look!" Ellie grabbed his arm. "Do you see what I see?"

Connor looked. "What am I supposed to be looking at?"

Ellie pointed.

Connor frowned. "So? All day workshop... all welcome...booking phone number..." He looked at her. "I don't get it."

Maybe she was mistaken. Ellie knew that she could get carried away sometimes. But now she'd spotted it she was sure it was worth a try.

"Don't you see? Where the singing workshop is being held? Today!" She pointed again, stabbing the word with her finger.

He looked again. "At the Coliseum." He looked back at her. "A coliseum? In London? Where is it...and *what* is it?"

Ellie shrugged and looked at the poster again. "Okay, it's spelled differently, but I think I've heard of it... Maybe it's some sort of theatre." She tugged at his sleeve. "You said he used to like singing. What if he didn't go to Rome at all, and is still in London? At this singing workshop thing. Is that the sort of thing he might do?"

Connor looked a bit shell-shocked, but he didn't take more than a few moments to gather his wits. "He might," he said slowly. "And if he *is* still in the city we've got a chance of finding him. So maybe I was worrying for no reason. If Joe was better at spelling I might have googled the right place and not jumped to the wrong conclusion. Does the poster give an address?"

"Yes, it does." Ellie unpinned the poster and took it over to the counter. "Would you mind if we had this?"

The assistant looked puzzled. "Help yourself. The workshop will be over soon anyway."

Connor joined in. "Excuse me. Is the Coliseum easy to get to?" he asked.

"Dunno," said the shop assistant. "It's not my sort of thing. But I don't think it's far."

Connor grabbed the poster from Ellie and dodged out of the shop. By the time she had caught up with him he was already hailing a cab.

"I think we could walk it," said Ellie as he yanked open the door of the cab that had pulled up to the curb. "The workshop doesn't end until five."

"Get in," he snarled. "I'm not taking any chances."

Ellie couldn't help giggling. It was like being

in an American cop film. "Calm down," she said as the cab pulled away.

"I am calm," Connor said, but he was obviously very, very angry.

"Connor."

"What?"

Ellie put her hand on his arm, afraid that he might throw it off, but he didn't. "If Joe *is* there, and you go storming up to him in this mood it's not going to help. He'll think you're as bad as his father."

"It would make me feel better though." There was a break in his voice. He turned away from her and stared out of the window.

It wasn't long before the cab pulled up. Ellie waited on the pavement while Connor paid the driver. When he joined her he looked up at the lovely old stone building. "Wow. It's amazing. Is that a globe on the top of it?" He took a deep breath and clutched Ellie's hand. "Come on, let's see if you've found him, shall we?"

Ellie almost felt as if she shouldn't be there. *Home of English National Opera* it said on one banner, and *Home of English National Ballet* on another. But Ellie didn't feel at home at all in these rarefied surroundings. Connor, on the other hand, didn't appear at all fazed. He showed the poster to the woman in the ticket office and asked directions, followed signs and pulled Ellie down corridors. At last, the sound of singing told them they were close. Connor pushed open the door, and there, at the far end of a large room was a collection of people. They were all ages, shapes and sizes, and they were all singing, and being conducted by a man standing in front of them. Connor and Ellie stood quietly, listening.

"Is he there?" she whispered after a moment.

Connor nodded. "Third from the left, at the back."

Ellie looked for her first glimpse of the elusive

Joe Steel. He was partly obscured by a rather large woman in front of him. But he was tall, and slim, very much like Connor, except he had his long brown hair tied back. He was singing as if his very life depended on it, and looked as if he was having a wonderful time.

When the conductor brought them to a stop, Joe exchanged a few words with the man to his left, and they both laughed. He looked quite at home.

Ellie glanced at Connor. Fortunately, he'd calmed down for the moment. At least, he didn't show any signs of going up to Joe and shouting at him, for which Ellie felt rather relieved. But just as she thought that, Connor started to walk quickly towards the group of singers. "What are you going to do?" she said.

He didn't answer. Maybe he hadn't heard her. Ellie hurried to catch him up, feeling totally out of her depth.

Joe was just responding to something the

woman in front of him had said to him, when he noticed Connor and Ellie. He looked startled. *Serves him right*, thought Ellie to herself. Joe muttered something, left the group, and hurried to intercept them. He glanced curiously at Ellie before trying to smile at Connor.

"Connor! I'm sorry. I was going to call and tell you when I'd be back, but we have to switch our phones off in here, and I forgot at lunchtime." He looked worried. "How did you find me?"

Connor just looked at him. Then he turned to Ellie. "Ellie, this is Joe. The person you thought you'd be interviewing."

Joe looked even more uncomfortable. "Sorry," he said again, this time to Ellie. "But I didn't ever really agree to an interview...it was my dad."

"Connor explained," said Ellie.

"Oh, well, *great*! So you understand. That's good." He glanced back at the singing group, and the conductor, who was looking in his direction. "I have to get back, but...can you wait for me? I'll be out at five."

Connor shrugged. "Well so far we've spent the whole day waiting for you," he said bitterly. "So I suppose we can wait a bit longer. No disappearing though, or that's you and me finished."

"No disappearing," Joe agreed, looking very grateful. "I promise. See you back here at five." He was already walking back to the group. "There's a café," he called back helpfully over his shoulder. "You could get a drink, or something."

"Yeah," growled Connor, sounding deeply unimpressed. "Thanks for your concern."

13

Sorting
it out

Connor refused to move more than a couple of metres away from the room where Joe was singing. "He's not getting away from me again," he growled when Ellie suggested they find something to eat. She could understand his concern, but it had been a long time since they'd eaten. She went in search of food while he sat on a chair halfway down the corridor. When she came back with sandwiches and drinks Connor was in a more reflective mood.

"I don't think I've been a very good friend to Joe," he said, as Ellie handed him his sandwich.

"What makes you say that?"

"Well, I didn't ask him if anything was wrong, I just complained at him when he sneaked off. I didn't think to ask why. I just thought he was being a pain. He must have thought he couldn't confide in me."

Ellie sighed. "You're not the only one who has made a bit of a mess of things," she said. "I fell out with my best friend just before she went on holiday and I haven't heard from her since."

Connor looked at her with sympathy. "That's tough," he said. "I hope you manage to sort it out."

"Me too," said Ellie, with feeling. "It can be hard work being a good friend." After that, neither of them said anything for a while.

Eventually, the door opened, and the singers emerged, chatting and laughing. Joe was one of the last to come out. The conductor was talking to him, and Joe was listening carefully. At last, the conductor handed Joe something, they shook hands and the conductor disappeared into another part of the building. The singers were leaving in twos and threes, but Joe had spotted Connor and Ellie and immediately came over to join them. He stood awkwardly in front of them and cleared his throat.

"Sorry," he said. "For messing both of you about."

Connor looked at him angrily. "I'm your best buddy," he said. "But you didn't tell me what was going on."

"I know. I'm sor—"

"Stop *saying* that!" Connor gave Joe a shove.

"Well maybe I would have told you if I'd thought you were interested," said Joe crossly. He shoved Connor back. "But you just kept going on about sightseeing."

"We're in *London*!" *Shove*. "I guess it's natural to want to see it." *Shove*.

Each shove was harder than the last, and finally Joe took a backwards step. Then, all of a sudden, Connor launched himself at Joe. Joe was slammed against the wall, and Ellie could hear him grunt as the air was expelled out of his lungs. "Oof!"

Sandwich wrappers and drinks bottles were scattered across the floor. Joe had hooked his foot around Connor's leg, and now they both toppled, wrestling, to the ground.

"Stop it!" said Ellie, scared that security would come and they'd get into trouble, but they showed no sign of hearing her.

After a minute, Joe seemed to be getting the upper hand, but just as he made to kneel on Connor's arms, Connor threw him off and the tables were turned. Now Connor was sitting on Joe's stomach with a bunch of his T-shirt in his hands. The fight seemed to have gone out of Joe. He lay there not moving, and for a moment or two they were both still, breathing heavily.

"Cry uncle?" asked Connor.

"Uncle," replied Joe as well as he could. To Ellie's relief that appeared to mean they were friends again. Connor got up, offered his hand and pulled Joe to his feet. Then Connor bent down to pick up a stray drinks bottle and Joe gave him a shove. Connor staggered but didn't quite fall. He turned round to look at Joe and they grinned at each other. The fight still seemed to be over, and the boys began to chat as if they'd never fallen out.

"I thought if I stayed with Dad this summer we could talk properly, and that he'd come round to understanding about me not wanting to join the band. But if anything he's been worse about it."

Connor nodded. "He isn't very good at listening."

Joe smiled. "I've got a secret weapon now though...or at least I hope I have."

"Really?" Connor and Ellie spoke at the

same time. Joe pulled a piece of paper out of his pocket and waved it at them.

"Yeah. You see, I've decided that it's no good fighting him. Dad just digs his heels in when I try to disagree with anything he wants me to do."

Connor looked puzzled. "But that means you'll have to do what he says."

Joe shook his head. "Not necessarily. I was talking to Mr. Edwards, the guy who took the singing workshop here today. He told me about a school I might be able to go to that trains singers. If I could get in, I could tell Dad that I want to improve my voice if I'm going to sing onstage. Hopefully he'll go for it, because the school has turned out some good rock musicians and singers. But secretly I'll be going on to train as an opera singer after I leave the school."

Connor stared at Joe. "Opera?"

Joe grinned. "I know. Crazy, isn't it? But I

like to sing. You know that, Connor. It's just that Dad's music doesn't do it for me. I saw an advert for this the other day when I disappeared." He looked sorry. "I just needed to get away for a bit. I was wandering around, feeling trapped by what Dad wants for me. Then I saw this workshop thing, and decided to go because I fancied trying something new... and I thought you'd laugh if I told you." He looked at his friend. "Sorry."

"That's okay," Connor told him. "I probably would have."

"Anyway, Mr. Edwards teaches classes at the school too, from time to time." Joe looked pleased. "He listened to me at lunchtime and said he thinks I've got a really good chance of getting in."

Connor was still staring. "But...*opera.*"

Joe looked defiant. "Heavy metal is okay. Dad's band is great...but it's not for me. I think I know what I want to do now, and in the end

I'll do it, whatever Dad says. You'll see. By the time I'm eighteen he won't be able to rule my life any more." He hesitated. "And I really hope that once he understands that it isn't so very different from what he does, he'll stop trying to bully me and start to be just a bit proud."

Connor shook his head. "Opera. It's like... *highbrow* stuff. How do you even understand it, let alone sing it?"

"It's not so very different from the school productions we used to do. It's just more... complex. And I *don't* sing it. Not yet anyway. Today was just a fun workshop. The real work will begin once I start voice training properly. I'll have some money of my own by then. So even if Dad refuses to pay, I'll still be able to do it. There's a load of money in trust for me, but I can't touch it until I'm eighteen."

He looked at the piece of paper in his hand. "It's called Rockley Park School. If only they'll take me! And if only Dad will let me go. I really fancy going to an English school for a year or two."

The name rang a bell in Ellie's head. "Rockley Park?"

Joe looked at her eagerly. "Do you know it?"

"No." She shook her head. "But I have heard of it. I interviewed Pop and Lolly Lowther a while ago. Have you heard of them? They both went there, and said they absolutely loved it."

Joe looked pleased. "Yeah. I've heard of them," he said. "They'll make Dad even more impressed about the school. Tell you what, Ellie, if I get in I'll give you an interview all about the school if you want. So long as you keep the opera idea a secret."

Ellie thought quickly. "It's a deal!" she said. "It would be great to be able to tell *Heart* readers a bit more about Rockley Park. And there'd be no better way to do it than by interviewing you. You have to promise me one thing though."

154

"What's that?"

"When you start training properly as an opera singer, you give me the scoop."

Joe laughed. "It's a deal. Once I'm able to make my own decisions, and get my first job, you'll be the first to know...except for Connor of course."

"And if he forgets, *I'll* let you know about it," said Connor firmly.

Just then, Ellie's phone bleeped. It was her mum. *Are you okay? Are you coming back for dinner? Don't be too late, will you?*

"I think I'm going to have to go home," she told the boys.

"But what about the other interview?" said Joe. "The one I let you down over."

"I didn't think you wanted to do that one," said Ellie in surprise.

"Well..." Joe scratched his head. "I don't want to talk in depth about how I feel about being Rocky Steel's son. I'm sure you can understand why. But could you do a sort of day in the life of Joe Steel? Would that be any use? Dad would love it if you came to a gig, so you'd be doing me a favour too. You could write about being backstage, and living in hotels...that sort of thing. What d'you think?"

"I'd have to run it past my Editor," mused Ellie, "but it sounds great to me, and I'd love to go to a gig. It would be fantastic!"

"Right then!" said Joe. "Let's set it up. I'll speak to Dad. You talk to your Editor and we'll see what we can do." A slow smile crept over his face. "And I'm sure Connor wouldn't mind coming to another gig if you're going to be there."

Connor blushed, and thumped Joe on his arm, but the boys were both smiling. Ellie liked Joe much more than she thought she would. And he was right. It *would* be especially good to be at the gig with Connor.

14

At the airport

Straight away on Monday morning, before the Steel Vortex gig, Ellie told Francesca the truth about her abortive Joe Steel interview, and of her new idea...a combined concert and interview article. Ellie was careful not to mention anything about Joe's problems with his father, or his very secret ambition.

"Well those two boys certainly gave you the runaround," said Francesca with a laugh. "But you seem to have come out of it rather well. A backstage article, with the boys, a description of the gig you're going to tonight, and a bit about Rocky Steel himself! That all sounds pretty good to me. Well done! Do the article straight away on Tuesday, while it's still all fresh in your mind. I'm sure Angel will go for it."

Steel Vortex were playing three gigs in London, and Rocky sent a car to pick Ellie up for the concert that Monday evening. Connor and Joe were there to greet her, and they took her backstage so she could interview both Rocky and Joe. Rocky was really nice to her, but she definitely got the feeling that it wouldn't be much fun to get on the wrong side of him.

"So is it a thrill, having such a cool father?" she asked Joe. She was certain Joe's father would approve of the question.

Joe smiled blandly. "Oh yes," he said, and she was almost sure that he was trying not to laugh. "It sure is!"

Heavy metal wasn't really Ellie's favourite sort of music, and there were lots of people of her mum's age in the audience, but none of that mattered. Live concerts were always exciting, and Steel Vortex certainly knew how to ramp up the atmosphere. Joe told her lots of technical details, and snippets of insider gossip about the band, which Ellie knew would make a great article. And Connor was there, which made the whole evening even more wonderful.

The next few days flew by. Connor met Ellie after work each day and they hung out together. Connor got his wish to go on the London Eye, as well as several other places. Sometimes Joe was with him and they all had fun together, but he was often busy having singing lessons with a teacher Mr. Edwards had recommended.

"Dad has said I can do an audition for Rockley Park," Joe told Ellie. "So I'm going to have as many lessons as I can."

"Was it difficult persuading him?" said Ellie.

Joe looked really happy. "He didn't like the thought of me going to school in England," he said. "But then he spoke to Mom on the phone and she *loved* the idea. She'd so like me to become more of a European! After all, I was born in England, but have hardly ever been here. Anyway, after that Dad spoke to a few friends and found out that several of them had good things to say about the school. It seems to have a great reputation for academic work, *and* for training great performers, and it's a boarding school, so they know I'll be looked after okay."

"The school we go to in the States doesn't specialize in music," chipped in Connor. "So this one will be much better for you." He frowned. "Though I'll miss you if you get in here."

"I'll be home in the vacations," said Joe. "If I get accepted that is."

"You'll get in," Connor said, "I bet you will."

"Fingers crossed," said Ellie.

With so much excitement Ellie had almost forgotten about Hannah coming home. Almost, but not quite. She hoped more and more to get a message from her, but still nothing turned up. She wondered if she ought to send another herself, but didn't want to push it. If Hannah wanted to get in touch she would.

Ellie was filled with equal amounts of anticipation and sadness the day before Hannah was due back. Anticipation, because she refused to give up hope for their friendship, and sadness, because on that same day, Connor, Joe and Rocky were flying off to Germany on the next leg of the tour.

She'd so enjoyed herself with the boys, but this was their last night together. Now it was getting late. They'd been out for a meal, and were going to hail a cab to take Ellie home.

"I've had a lovely time," she told them wistfully as they stood in the warm night air, waiting for a cab to come by. "The gig was fun, you gave me material for a great article, Joe, and, well..." She turned to Connor. "I'm so glad I met you at the hotel that day."

"Me too," said Connor.

"And keep in touch, both of you," she added. "Let me know about Rockley Park. I'll have all my fingers and toes crossed for you."

"Thanks," said Joe, giving her a big hug. "Thanks for being a good friend."

"I don't know about that," she mumbled into his T-shirt, hugging him back.

Joe caught sight of a cab as he let her go and stepped out to flag it down. While he did that, Connor took the opportunity to give her a hug himself. "You'll text me, won't you?" he said. "And you'll find me on Facebook?"

"Yes," she said, feeling near to tears. "Of course I will."

"And don't worry about your friend tomorrow. If Joe and I can make up I'm sure you and Hannah can!"

There was no time for anything else. The cab was there, and the door was open. She climbed in and Connor closed the door. Ellie fumbled to put her seat belt on, feeling bereft already. The last she saw of them was Connor's face, looking as sad as she felt, waving until the cab went round the corner. Then the boys were right out of sight.

Sunday morning came much too soon. What with missing Connor and being worried about seeing Hannah again Ellie really didn't want to go with her mum to pick Hannah and her parents up from the airport. It would be a squash in the car, and if they weren't going to be friends again it would be *awful,* but Georgia seemed to be totally confident that things would be fine between them.

"Skulking at home while I collect her family won't help anything," she said to Ellie. "You have to face things in life, not run away from them. You have nothing to be ashamed of, and you still want to be friends. If Hannah feels differently that's up to her, but don't behave as if she doesn't like you any more. That's just silly."

Ellie was sure Connor would be against her skulking too, so she made her mind up to go, and to hope for the best. Besides, airports were exciting, even if you weren't flying anywhere. Ellie loved watching passengers arriving from far-flung places, especially Africa. Some of the people from that continent wore such colourful clothes. They made Westerners look unbelievably dowdy.

Luckily, the flight landed in the middle of the day, so Ellie didn't have to get up at the crack of dawn, which was just as well, after the late night she'd had. The airport wasn't far, and they were in good time to meet the flight. Ellie went to look at the arrivals board and frowned. "It's been delayed," she said to her mum.

"That's annoying," said Georgia. "How silly of me. I meant to check online before we set off, but I forgot."

"It's only half an hour," said Ellie. "We can go and have a coffee while we're waiting."

They watched the arrivals screen from one of the airport cafés, and soon the status of Hannah's flight turned to "landed". Ten minutes later, Ellie got a text.

Hi! it said. *Are you at the airport?* It was the first text Hannah had sent her since their argument.

Ellie replied. *Yes.* She wasn't sure what else to say, but her heart started to thump.

A few minutes later another came in. *Just hanging around for our bags. Can't wait to see you!*

Ellie heaved a huge sigh of relief. Maybe it would be all right. *Me too!* she replied, with her heart lifting. "Come on, Mum," she said to Georgia. "Let's go to arrivals. I expect they'll be through soon."

At the barrier there were lots of people waiting. Ellie found a space and leaned on the barrier, watching for people who looked as if they'd been on holiday. It didn't take long. They were unmistakable in their flip-flops and colourful clothes, bulging bags and tanned faces. Some of them looked as if they'd actually come straight from the beach.

Ellie saw Hannah before Hannah noticed Ellie. She was wearing a new pair of cool gold sandals, and had a short dress on that Ellie hadn't seen before. On her head was a straw hat. Her luggage was piled on a trolley, and her dad was pushing it, accompanied by her mum. They all looked very tanned and happy. For a moment Ellie regretted not going with them. It would have been such fun, and they would have come home with a huge number of shared happy memories. But then she remembered how she'd have been letting *Heart* down at the last minute, and how unprofessional that would have been. And in fact she'd done so much over the past few days; quite enough to make up for missing a foreign holiday! And then Hannah saw her, and let out a squeal of delight.

As soon as they hugged they both knew that everything was all right. "I'm sorry I was so horrible," breathed Hannah. "The longer I left it the harder it was to make contact. But I so hoped you'd be here."

"I'm sorry I let you down," said Ellie, and they hugged again.

"I got you such a sweet sun top," Hannah was saying as they walked slowly, arms linked, towards the exit. Then Ellie saw someone she recognized.

"Connor!" She disentangled her arm from Hannah's and muttered, "Hang on a minute," before he reached her.

He stood a couple of feet away from her, looking suddenly rather shy. "The others have gone through to departures," he explained. "But I saw the flight coming in from Malaga and hoped it might be the one you were meeting." He paused. "Everything all right then?"

Ellie nodded. "Everything's fine," she told him. "I'll introduce you..." She started to turn back to Hannah, but Connor grabbed her hand.

"Haven't got time," he said. "I just wanted to see if you were okay, and say goodbye again."

"Oh, okay."

For a couple of seconds they stood looking at each other; then he took hold of her shoulders and gave her a kiss, followed by the biggest bear hug she'd ever had in her entire life. "Don't forget," he said seriously. "This isn't really goodbye. I'll see you online tonight. Right?"

"Right," she said.

He took a deep breath. "Right," he said. He caught her hands, gave them a squeeze, and then, in an instant he was gone, lost in the throng of people. Ellie took a deep breath too, and turned back to Hannah. She was staring at her friend, open-mouthed.

"Wow! Ellie," she said, looking deeply impressed. "We've got an awful lot to catch up on!"

It was autumn. The leaves were beginning to turn in the park and Ellie and Hannah were back at school. The new copy of *Heart* was just out, and the girls were in Ellie's bedroom, flicking through it. Hannah had already read and admired the article on Joe Steel, and had heard all about the events leading up to it. Now, she had flipped to the quiz page.

"Let's do this," she said, scrabbling for a pen in her bag. "What's it about this month?"

"Friendship," said Ellie quietly. "I compiled it."

Hannah stopped looking for a pen. "You did? No way!" For a moment she looked uncertain, as the memory of their fractured friendship flickered across her face. Then she smiled warmly at Ellie. "In that case, shall we just read it together?"

Ellie nodded.

"Question one," read Hannah. *"Your best friend asks you at short notice to go on holiday with her and her parents, but you've got commitments at home."*

She looked at Ellie, but Ellie couldn't return her gaze. She was suddenly really worried that the quiz would reawaken all the problems they'd had in the summer. But it was okay. In fact it was more than okay. Hannah gave her a hug. That time was in the past, and they were firmer friends than ever. They went right through the quiz, and to their delight found that they would have chosen all the same answers. Then they got to the end.

"Last question." Hannah's voice was serious. *"What makes for the longest-lasting friendships?*

A. You'll do anything she suggests.

B. You don't just get on, you really understand each other's needs.

Or C. You go to the same school."

Hannah abandoned the magazine and gave Ellie a hug. "B," she said. "B, B, B every time. Now and for ever."

"Now and for ever," said Ellie.

For wannabe journalist, Ellie, doing work experience at her fave teen magazine is a dream come true. Check out the other titles in this stylish series:

A dream come true

Ellie's got a jealous rival who's determined to turn her dream job into a nightmare...

My life behind the scenes at...

Heart
Magazine

Boys, blues & shoes

Cindy Jefferies

ISBN: 9781409520214

Boys, blues & shoes

Ellie thinks she's going to miss out on meeting her
favourite band – until she finds herself on a photo
shoot with some very special 'extras'...

ISBN: 9781409520221

Search for a star

Can the Editor's pampered pooch help Ellie track down the star she'd love to interview?

Cindy Jefferies is the author of the fabulous

Fame School

Look out for:

Reach for the Stars
Rising Star
Secret Ambition
Rivals!
Tara's Triumph
Lucky Break
Solo Star
Christmas Stars
Pop Diva
Battle of the Bands
Star Maker
Dancing Star
Summer Spectacular
Trick or Treat

For more stylish reads
check out
www.fiction.usborne.com